Once he was staring at them—a sea of yellow canisters, each with an electronic detonator affixed—he was almost taken aback by just how many the Russian had managed to capture and move. The hall was filled with them, and there was no doubt in Bolan's mind that the explosions awaiting each were more than enough to produce a toxic cloud of incredible size. Based on the intelligence the Farm had provided, this number of canisters would be enough to poison almost the entire city.

He heard approaching footsteps and raised the Beretta.

"Beautiful, is it not?" The captain stepped into view. He was dressed in loose clothing in the local Javanese style. He held an electronic detonator in his hand.

"Place the detonator on the floor," Bolan said, his Beretta trained on the man.

"This is a standoff," the Russian said, laughing. "At least until I decide I wish to die. And then I will push this button and the entire city of Semarang dies with me."

MACK BOLAN ®
The Executioner

The Executioner®
Don Pendleton's

DANGEROUS TIDES

A GOLD EAGLE BOOK FROM

WORLDWIDE®

TORONTO • NEW YORK • LONDON
AMSTERDAM • PARIS • SYDNEY • HAMBURG
STOCKHOLM • ATHENS • TOKYO • MILAN
MADRID • WARSAW • BUDAPEST • AUCKLAND

Recycling programs
for this product may
not exist in your area.

First edition August 2009

ISBN-13: 978-0-373-64369-1

Special thanks and acknowledgment to
Phil Elmore for his contribution to this work.

DANGEROUS TIDES

Printed in U.S.A.

There is nothing so desperately monotonous as the sea, and I no longer wonder at the cruelty of pirates.
—James Russell Lowell
1819–1891

There are many reasons a man hoists the black flag and takes what he wants. When he does, he's not a romantic figure or a pirate. He's a predator and he's going to pay for his crimes.
—Mack Bolan

THE
MACK BOLAN

LEGEND

Nothing less than a war could have fashioned the destiny of the man called Mack Bolan. Bolan earned the Executioner title in the jungle hell of Vietnam.

But this soldier also wore another name—Sergeant Mercy. He was so tagged because of the compassion he showed to wounded comrades-in-arms and Vietnamese civilians.

Mack Bolan's second tour of duty ended prematurely when he was given emergency leave to return home and bury his family, victims of the Mob. Then he declared a one-man war against the Mafia.

He confronted the Families head-on from coast to coast, and soon a hope of victory began to appear. But Bolan had broken society's every rule. That same society started gunning for this elusive warrior—to no avail.

So Bolan was offered amnesty to work within the system against terrorism. This time, as an employee of Uncle Sam, Bolan became Colonel John Phoenix. With a command center at Stony Man Farm in Virginia, he and his new allies—Able Team and Phoenix Force—waged relentless war on a new adversary: the KGB.

But when his one true love, April Rose, died at the hands of the Soviet terror machine, Bolan severed all ties with Establishment authority.

Now, after a lengthy lone-wolf struggle and much soul-searching, the Executioner has agreed to enter an "arm's-length" alliance with his government once more, reserving the right to pursue personal missions in his Everlasting War.

1

The SH-60B Seahawk helicopter churned purposefully out of the sky, dropping perilously close to the water and raising a wake in the already rough seas below. The chopper's twin engines pushed it through the twilight at the urging of Jack Grimaldi, Stony Man pilot and long-time friend of Mack Bolan, the Executioner. Grimaldi imagined he could feel the spray of seawater on the helicopter's belly as he skimmed the waves.

"We're coming up on the insertion point, Sarge!" Grimaldi said into his throat mike.

Behind him, in the open bay of the Seahawk, Mack Bolan lowered a pair of anti-fog goggles over his eyes. Then he checked the fit of the Boker Orca dive knife strapped to his thigh over his wet suit. He had already verified that the watertight pack strapped to the small of his back was double-buckled and secure. It was almost time to leave his headset—and Grimaldi's chopper—behind.

"Understood, Jack," he acknowledged, keying his own mike. "Final checklist."

"Gear?" Grimaldi said.

"Secure."

"Plumett case?"

The Executioner checked the seals on the heavy black case, then slung it over his shoulder and across his back.

"On board."

"Air supply?" Grimaldi asked.

Bolan checked the fit of the mouthpiece on the modified pony bottle he wore on his chest. The bottle was fixed to one of the shoulder straps of his backpack, cinched tightly in place with nylon webbing. The small gauge on the high-tech bottle read Full.

"Check," Bolan said.

"DPV?" Grimaldi ticked off.

Bolan reached down and switched on the standby power of the electric, self-contained Driver Propulsion Vehicle Stony Man Farm had provided for him. The muted status LEDs were all green. The mounted GPS locator displayed his position relative to his target coordinates. The DPV was a sealed electric motor with a single-use power supply, essentially a giant propeller cylinder and rudder assembly. Twin joysticks jutted above and behind, containing triggers to adjust the throttle and steer the unit.

"Ready," Bolan said.

"Good luck, Sarge," Grimaldi said. "And good hunting." The cocky pilot turned all business as he watched his instruments. "On my mark, Striker," he said, using Bolan's Stony Man code name. "Five…four…three…two…one…*mark.*"

At Grimaldi's signal, Bolan pulled off his headset and shoved the DPV out of the chopper, the twin sticks of the machine tight in his fists. He hit the water below like a stone. The heavy device pulled him beneath the roiling waves. He paused as he descended, orienting himself and taking air from the pony bottle, watching in the darkness as the GPS unit pointed the way to his destination.

Bolan thumbed the machine's controls and held on tightly as the almost-silent device began pulling him rapidly through the water. He adjusted course with a few taps of the right-hand trigger, managing his depth by angling the DPV and his body with it.

Above him, Grimaldi would be piloting the Seahawk back to the *Perry*-class frigate *James Richardson*. The firepower available to Bolan and to Stony Man was considerable, but no amount of heavy weaponry could do the job that now faced him. No, to succeed, Bolan would have to use stealth, mounting a soft probe into enemy-held territory in order to liberate innocent men and women.

It was an all too common scenario for the Executioner.

Bolan had covered a lot of ground in the past several hours, first by jet, then by helicopter, then on the frigate, only to take to the skies once more to be dropped into the cold sea below. It had started with a single telephone call, routed to Bolan through channels from Washington by way of Stony Man Farm. The circuits connecting them were complex, but the scrambled phone briefing from Hal Brognola—speaking to Bolan from the big Fed's Justice Department office in D.C.—had been straightforward enough.

"A cruise ship has been hijacked," Brognola had said without preamble.

The natural assumption in the modern age was that yet another terrorist group was claiming responsibility for yet another act of violence against helpless men, women and children. Brognola quickly explained that the problem was, if anything, even more serious.

"What we have," the big Fed said, "is an act of piracy."

"Pirates?" Bolan had not been sure he'd heard correctly.

"It's a growing and very serious issue in certain parts of the world," Brognola said. "As you know, pirate attacks off the cost of Africa have surged, cutting off aid to countries like Somalia. The South China Sea alone, which sees a third of worldwide commercial shipping, sees about half of the pirate attacks recorded by the International Maritime Bureau every year. We're talking about a cost to cargo insurers upwards of a hundred million U.S. dollars a year."

"Big business," Bolan agreed.

"And getting worse," Brognola said. "It's not just Africa and other backwaters. Nobody's immune." He paused. "Our friends the Chinese executed over a dozen Chinese pirates not too long ago, after convicting them of murdering the crew of a freighter near Hong Kong waters. Without doubt, however, the worst pirate activity is in Indonesia. Malaysia, Singapore and Indonesia all patrol the Malacca Strait," Brognola went on, "which is one of the world's busiest shipping lanes. But they can't be everywhere."

"What's the profile of the attacks?" Bolan asked.

"The pirates have historically targeted commercial shipping vessels, but they're branching out. Now we're seeing civilian tourists targeted. A couple of years ago, an American cruise ship was attacked in Somali waters by pirates in speedboats who fired machine guns and an RPG at the larger ship."

"I remember that. Didn't they use some kind of sonic weapon to defend themselves?"

"A long-range acoustic device," Brognola said. "The LRAD supposedly helped drive off the pirates, but there's debate about just how effective it was. In reality the ship rammed one of the pirate boats and ground it under her bow. That was enough to do the job."

"So what's happening now?" Bolan asked.

"It's terrorism and that's all it is. The motive may be financial rather than political, but they're the same enemies you've faced down time and again."

"What are the details?" Bolan asked.

"The *Duyfken Ster,*" Brognola said. "Holland registry, part of a cruise line that operates regularly in Indonesia, is now in the hands of pirates. The ship was taken off the coast of Java after making port in Semarang."

"How did they do it?"

"The reports are a little sketchy," Brognola said, "but at least a dozen men, maybe more, in two high-speed launchers, came at the ship from either side and boarded her using grapples. They swarmed the bridge, we believe, and established armed control over the rest of the ship. As you can imagine, there was no real resistance. Using the ship's radio, they've relayed a demand to shore."

"What do they want?"

"Money," Brognola said. "And lots of it. They've threatened to kill the passengers if they see any overt show of force."

"So what's our involvement?" Bolan said.

"A couple of the passengers are connected," Brognola said. "Family members of a U.S. congressman were taking the cruise. While officially the U.S. has done nothing but condemn the taking of the ship, much less acknowledge that the pirates have lucked in to high-value hostages…unofficially, the president wants these pirates taken down, and hard."

"Why no official involvement?" Bolan asked.

"The usual reasons," Brognola sighed. "Territoriality. Issues of sovereignty. Stubborn pride. None of the local governments involved wants to admit it is not capable of solving the pirate problem, even though the situation is widely known to be out of control. If we come in and mop it up for them, we'll have shamed them on the world stage. The U.S. isn't well-liked in that corner of the world, of course, and we've been told, more or less politely, to mind our own damned business."

"Even if lives are at stake?"

"You know as well as I do, Striker, that political expedience is always going to trump human life."

"Not for me," Bolan said. "Never for me."

"And not for the Farm," Brognola nodded. "The Man has given us his blessing. We need results. And we need them quickly and quietly."

"Then let's do it," Bolan had agreed.

Several hours and a few thousand miles later, the Executioner held tightly to the control sticks of the DPV, the wake churned by the machine's motor beating an almost pleasant staccato against his wet suit-clad chest. His waterproof pack tugged against its straps. He was making good time and, according to the GPS unit on the DPV, he was exactly on course.

It did not take long for the preprogrammed coordinates—updated every few seconds as Stony Man Farm coordinated real-time satellite surveillance overhead—to match Bolan's GPS-tracked location. The soldier paused to input a brief set of commands on the DPV's keypad. Using the electronic locator, he oriented the DPV and pressed the key.

The little machine whirred quickly away, freed of Bolan's two-hundred-plus pounds of man and equipment. Bolan watched it disappear into the murky darkness of the underwater world before kicking with his feet, pushing himself toward the surface.

The Executioner let his face mask, then his head, break the surface as he took in his surroundings. The stern of the giant cruise ship loomed ominously above him in the moonlight. He waited, quietly treading water, counting off the numbers in his head.

The shock wave, when it came, was not terribly large, but he could feel it nonetheless. The explosives packed into the nose of the DPV obliterated the machine at its preset coordinates, just off the bow of the ship. The charge was designed to produce as much noise and light as possible while posing little risk to the ship itself.

As the bomb blew, Bolan reached back over his shoulder and released the seal on the Plumett case. The heavy Plumett AL-54 he carried had been tuned and modified by the Farm's armorer, John "Cowboy" Kissinger. Its range was more than adequate for the task. Floating in the water, Bolan lined up the launcher on one of the struts of the deck openings above the shipboard marina. He fired.

He could hear shouting from somewhere forward on the ship as the lightweight carbon fiber grapnel hit its mark, the Plumett's 8 mm polyester rope streaming behind it. Without hesitation, Bolan pulled the quick release, letting the Plumett case fall away. He scrambled up the polyester line hand over hand, his traction-surfaced wet-suit gloves providing purchase as he went.

Bolan landed as quietly as he could. He released the waterproof gear bag and began removing its contents, methodically and efficiently gearing up after he removed his flippers. The combat harness inside the bag contained a holster and magazine pouches for his Kissinger-tuned Beretta 93-R machine pistol, which rode in its custom shoulder holster with sound suppressor attached. Over the right thigh of his wet suit, Bolan strapped on a rig for his .44 Magnum Desert Eagle. Spare magazines rode in the belt pouches on the black web belt he clipped around his waist. Also in a pouch on his waist was a knurled aluminum combat flashlight.

Bolan took out waterproof, no-slip synthetic moccasins to cover his feet. They would give him silent traction on the cruise ship's decks. The last item he removed was his ruggedized PDA phone, the muted face of which he illuminated briefly. According to the plans in the PDA, he was on Deck 3, above the ship's raised marina. When the steel mesh enclosure of the marina was lowered to form a pool, guests on the cruise ship could use that to swim in the sea and also avail themselves of the Zodiacs, water skis and sailboats kept on hand. But partying on the water was the last thing on the minds of those trapped aboard the vessel. Bolan was keenly aware of the presence of innocents on board, all around him. He drew the Beretta and press-checked it to verify that a 124-grain subsonic hollow point round was chambered.

The soldier pulled the grapnel free from its position wrapped around a railing strut. He hooked it through the empty gear bag and tossed both over the side so they would not be found and give away his presence prematurely. Then he stalked forward.

He made his way through the ship's galley, which was dark and smelled of spoiled food. He dared not risk using the flashlight he carried, as it would give away his position to anyone lurking nearby. Instead he crept among the counters, half-crouched, threading his way past fallen pots and pans and puddles of alcohol dotted with broken glass.

There were bullet holes in some of the bulkheads. Dried blood coated the floor and made a grisly path toward one of the walk-in coolers. Bolan had no doubt he would find bodies inside. Either the pirates had felt it necessary to make an example of some of the crew, or even the passengers, or they had met resistance and snuffed it out. Either way, it was likely the cooler was now a morgue. The Executioner passed it by, knowing there was nothing he could do for those already dead.

Moving silently, Bolan paused just outside the entrance to the galley. Through the open hatchway he could smell tobacco. There was a sentry out there. Pressing himself against the bulkhead, his back flat on the painted metal, he leveled the Beretta 93-R across his chest. Then he took his left hand, balled it into a fist and simply knocked on the bulkhead.

He tapped three times, waited and tapped again.

"Budi?" a voice asked, uncertain. The sentry called Budi's name twice more before asking something in what Bolan assumed was Indonesian. Finally, Bolan rapped on the wall yet again.

"Budi!" the sentry said angrily. Bolan listened as the man walked to the entrance and stepped through.

"Sorry, Budi's not here," Bolan whispered. The startled sentry turned to look at him, a Kalashnikov held in his hands, ready to open fire. Bolan triggered a single suppressed round from the Beretta. The head shot dropped the terrorist, dead before he hit the deck. Bolan snatched the AK-74 before it could clatter to the floor.

Several seconds passed as Bolan waited, listening. There was no more movement from beyond the galley. Holstering the Beretta, he placed the terrorist's weapon on the deck and quickly searched the corpse. He found nothing of use—a spare magazine for the Kalashnikov, a Pakistani-made folding knife, a few loose coins from countries in the region. It took only a moment to drag the sentry to the galley's cooler. He was not surprised to find it filled with corpses, most of them dressed as cooks and shipboard stewards. Bolan added the pirate to the pile and secured the cooler door.

Scooping up the Kalashnikov, Bolan popped the cover. He pulled the bolt, recoil spring and plunger assembly free, hiding the now-useless rifle behind a metal garbage bin. He dropped the parts inside the bin itself. There was no sense leaving functioning weapons behind. It was a lesson he'd learned on the many battlefields he'd walked through the years.

Satisfied, Bolan continued on, through the bowels of the

ship, determined to free the passengers. The pirates had expected two hundred or more soft targets, plus the crew. He was going to give them a lot more than they'd bargained for.

The Executioner had come aboard.

Hell was coming with him.

2

A sweep of the ship's luxury restaurant yielded nothing. The faint smell of food starting to spoil filled the air. Many of the place settings held half-finished meals, glasses of wine overturned, leaving red stains across the white linen tablecloths. Here and there were pools of dried blood and bullet holes. The pirates had not gone easily with the passengers or the ship's crew. That much was obvious.

Bolan crept through the restaurant and checked his bearings. Beyond the restaurant, the remainder of this deck—to the bow—held officers' quarters. There was also a medical facility. Bolan found that and checked it first, finding some of the supplies scattered around, the drawers and cabinets emptied. A few empty plastic bottles littered the floor. Bolan picked one up. It was a prescription painkiller, from the label. The pirates must have gone through and swept up anything with narcotic value, of which there would be plenty among medical stores. From the mess made of some of the first-aid supplies, it was possible that one or more of the invaders had been wounded during the attack. Either that, or they'd allowed medical treatment to be given to wounded crew or passengers. There was no way to be sure yet.

As he stalked through the officers' cabins, Bolan paused at each hatchway, listening. When he heard nothing, he moved on to the next, and repeated the process as he moved through the section. He was getting close to the bow when he heard muffled cries from one of the cabins. He stopped, the Beretta 93-R steady in his grip, as he assessed the situation.

A woman cried out, her voice muted by something, most likely a gag. There was the sound of a hand slapping flesh, and another cry of pain from the woman. Then a man's voice, saying something angrily—Bolan was certain it was in Vietnamese; a language with which he'd had some experience—followed by a second voice, in broken English.

Bolan waited as long as he dared, as the two men laughed and again struck the woman. He gritted his teeth. When the man speaking in English said, "Let's finish with her," he knew he had no more time to assess the threat.

The Executioner used his left shoulder to shove the partially open door the rest of the way, launching himself through the hatchway with gun in hand. As he hit the floor and rolled on his leading shoulder, he quickly surveyed the room. On the bunk against one bulkhead, two men held a young woman, wearing only her underwear. One had a kitchen knife, possibly taken from the galley. An ancient Tokarev pistol had been left on the small metal writing desk nearby. The pirates—both of them dark skinned and clad in mismatched camouflage fatigues—looked up in disbelief as the intruder tumbled into the small cabin.

That look of disbelief was all one of them would ever wear again. The man with the knife got out a single curse in Vietnamese before a 124-grain hollow point from Bolan's Beretta silenced him forever, snapping his head back as he crumpled onto the bunk. The knife clattered to the deck.

The second pirate was smarter and faster. He threw himself at Bolan, probably realizing he had no other chance. The smaller man slammed into the soldier, knocking him back against the writing desk, one hand scrabbling at the desk as the other locked a viselike grip on Bolan's gun hand. Even as he grappled with the pirate, Bolan knew the man was going for the unattended Tokarev.

Bolan had greater upper-body strength, but the pirate fought like a madman, fear of death and surging adrenaline lending strength to his desperate efforts. Bolan managed to lock his elbow around the pirate's free arm, effectively stopping his attempts to grab for the Tokarev. Then he slammed a series of vicious knee jabs into the pirate's gut. The man cried out and bent over, losing his hold on Bolan's wrist. The soldier immediately clubbed the pirate on the back of the head with the Beretta. The man went limp and Bolan allowed him to collapse to the floor.

The woman on the bunk began to sob into her gag. Her eyes were wide and moved from Bolan to the dead man beside her, then back to Bolan again.

"It's all right," Bolan said softly. "I'm not going to hurt you." From a small pouch on his web gear he produced a flat roll of black fabric tape and two plastic strap cuffs. He used the tape to gag the unconscious pirate. Then he used the cuffs to secure the smaller man's ankles and cuffed the wrists behind the man's back.

Once the prisoner was secured, the Executioner turned to the distraught woman. Bolan judged her age at early twenties, at most. Smeared makeup and tangled blond hair did not hide her good looks. The pirates had obviously known what they wanted when they picked her out of the crowd. Bolan eased closer to her, slowly, careful not to startle her.

"I'm going to remove that," he said as he reached for her gag, his tone calm and reassuring. He was no stranger to dealing with the victims of crimes such as the one he had just averted. "Don't cry out when I do, please. Everything is going to be all right."

The woman let him take off the gag. She froze for a moment, then threw herself at him, shaking uncontrollably, trying and failing to choke back deep, wracking sobs. Bolan, the Beretta still in one hand, hooked one arm around her and let her cry. "My name is Cooper," he said, using his Justice Department alias. "Matt Cooper. I'm here to stop what is happening."

The woman sobbed something against his chest. It took Bolan a moment to realize she was saying something coherent. "The…the lounge," she managed to utter.

"What lounge?" Bolan asked.

"Deck…deck five, and six," she stammered. "The big lounge with the casino. They've got them…got them all there."

"The hostages?" Bolan asked. The young woman nodded. "All right. What's your name?"

"Kris…Kristen."

"All right, Kristen," Bolan said. She had recovered enough to realize she was half naked. She found her clothes, which were rumpled but intact, and quickly dressed. Bolan turned away and checked the bound pirate once more, making certain he was still out and not playing possum. Then he reached out and beckoned to her, careful to keep his expression and his body language neutral.

"Where are we going?" Kristen asked, clearly terrified.

"To another part of this deck," Bolan said. "These are officers' quarters. We're going to find you another room. You'll lock yourself inside and stay there. Don't come out unless I come back for you or you hear a rescue team on the ship. All right?"

Kristen nodded, eyes still wide. After locking the unconscious pirate in the cabin and tucking away the pistol he'd recovered, Bolan took the woman by the hand and led her forward, listening carefully and moving as quietly as he could. Kristen, in bare feet, made no sound as they walked. The soldier finally found quarters that looked suitable and checked to make sure the door could be securely locked from the inside.

"You're going to leave me here?" Kristen asked.

"Don't worry," Bolan said. "This will all be over soon. Stay inside, make no sound and leave the door locked no matter what you do. Can you do that?"

"Yes…I think so."

"Good," Bolan said. "Lock the door now."

He waited as she did so. Then he found the nearest companionway and took it to the next deck. Deck 4, according to the details in his PDA, was roughly two-thirds guest cabins forward and amidships, with more officers' accommodations aft. Before he could approach Deck 5 and the casino lounge, Bolan would have to sweep Deck 4 for hostiles—and he would have to do it silently. He could not afford to alert the pirates guarding the hostages, nor could he risk having enemies approach from below when he did make his raid on the lounge.

Time, he knew, was precious. There was a chance the pirates he'd taken out would be missed, even discovered. He would have to take his battlefront to the enemy before that happened, to retain the element of surprise.

With the Beretta 93-R in his fist, its sound suppressor firmly in place, Bolan slipped wraithlike among the cabins of Deck 4. For the most part, the area seemed deserted. Bolan had checked almost all of the guest cabins—in some cases finding clothing and other belongings strewn about, as if searched none too gently by pirates looking for valuables—until he found one where two men were sleeping.

The first pirate had passed out on a sofa in the suite's small living area. Empty champagne bottles littered the carpeted deck around him. A second snored loudly in the bedroom beyond. There was no telling why, on a ship full of empty cabins, these two were sharing living space. The most likely explanation was that they'd been partying with booze taken from the ship's stores. Bolan knelt silently over the emaciated, Indonesian man, who wore a pair of cut-off cargo pants and clutched a beat-up rifle. The man awoke startled and struggled to aim his weapon. Sliding the knife quietly from its sheath, the Executioner drew it across the man's throat. He had no choice. The man had to be dealt with before he could raise an alarm.

The Executioner slipped into the suite's bedroom and found the snoring pirate. The man was Asian, dressed in a dirty tank top and jeans. A machete had been left on the floor next to the bed. Bolan saw, then, that the bedclothes were stained with blood. Someone had died there, and died hard. Bolan's features creased grimly as he looked down at the sleeping predator.

The man's eyes fluttered open. As he opened his mouth to shout, Bolan let the knife in his right hand fall. While the blade was still in the air, his fingers found the butt of the suppressed Beretta. The weapon cleared leather with a practiced movement. As the muzzle came on target, Bolan's finger took up the slack on the trigger, the entire motion smooth, fluid and fast. The 9 mm slug punched through the pirate's open mouth and ended his cry before the shout could escape his lungs.

The Executioner wasted no time. He searched the bodies, again finding nothing useful. Then he stripped the bolt from the rifle and left it in a wastebasket in the suite's bathroom. Finally, he retrieved his knife, cleaned it and sheathed it.

He was back on the hunt, moving from cabin to cabin, listening for movement and carefully, quietly checking each chamber. He could not leave anyone, could not risk discovery. The operation hinged on clearing Deck 4 before he made his run on Deck 5.

He checked his ruggedized PDA once more as he reached the aft third of the deck, the change in décor and the signs warning "crew only" telling him he was once more exploring officers' quarters. He had checked only two of these, finding them ransacked and devoid of personnel, when he found the first of the canisters.

The waist-high metal cylinder was bright yellow and emblazoned with chemical and biohazard warnings in Cyrillic. The warnings looked as if they had been spray-painted on recently. They were much more clear than the fading paint on the scarred metal tanks themselves. Bolan had enough experience with the language—and what the words on the canisters represented—to know he was dealing with something very dangerous. He found several more canisters in more of the unoccupied cabins. Unlike the first few, however, these had electronic devices of some kind attached to them, blinking green LEDs on each device indicating they were active and possibly armed.

They were detonators.

The engagement had suddenly become something much more than a simple hijacking. Bolan used the built-in camera in his wireless PDA, capturing digital images of the canisters and close-ups of the electronic detonators. He transmitted these to Stony Man Farm immediately, relying on the satellite encryption built into the device to safeguard the intelligence he was providing. He would have to risk the transmission itself. It was unlikely the pirates had the kind of sophisticated gear that could detect outgoing wireless phone signals, satellite or otherwise, but it was not impossible. Given the weapons of mass destruction he was now standing among, they could have anything. He would take the gamble in order to learn precisely what he was dealing with, if possible. Hundreds of lives could depend on it.

Bolan completed his count of the canisters and began to work his way back to the companionway that would take him to the next deck. Until he heard from the Farm he could do nothing but continue. He was about to check his weapons once more before ascending when he heard the faintest noise behind him.

The soldier whirled and ducked as he did so. The machete sang through the air and crashed against the metal bulkhead. Bolan brought the Beretta up and just as quickly lost it; a savage, numbing blow slammed into his wrist and sent the pistol flying onto the deck.

Bolan reacted instantly, pistoning a powerful front kick into his opponent. The blow took his opponent in the stomach, doubling him over and sending him back. Bolan crouched and ripped the knife free from its sheath as the pirate he faced struck a pose with a machete. The chipped and well-used blade glinted in the corridor lights.

"That's right, bad man," the pirate said. "I got your ass, just me."

"You're American," Bolan said, genuinely surprised. The man in front of him was easily six foot five and three hundred pounds, a muscled monster of a man. He wore a torn desert camouflage BDU blouse with the sleeves cut off and stained blue jeans tucked into U.S. Army-issue combat boots.

"That's right, for whatever that shit means," the man said, his teeth very white in his scarred, dark-skinned face. "I was in Iraq, man."

"And now you're a pirate?" Bolan said. Keeping the man talking was the only way to buy time. He could not afford to have the pirate alert the others before he was ready to free the hostages. Strangely, the man facing off against him seemed to have no urge to do so. Quite the contrary, in fact. The pirate looked relaxed, even pleased.

"I been bored a long while," the American pirate said. When he smiled the scar creasing his forehead and left cheek turned his features feral. "Don't go in for the rape-and-pillage act. Ain't no sex offender, man."

"You're as much a part of this as the others," Bolan said. "You're a traitor to your nation." He moved slightly, testing the pirate's reactions. The big man shifted a bit but remained calm, his fingers flexing on the handle of his machete.

"Don't matter what you think," the pirate scoffed. "I fought for my country. And what did I get when I got home? A big fat bag of nothing, man. And a nasty letter telling me they could call me back up anytime they felt like, even though I did my tour! I ain't nobody's slave, man. First chance I got I was out of there."

"To take up with murderers and hijackers," Bolan said.

"Kicked around from place to place a while." The man began to circle Bolan in the corridor, forcing the Executioner to move to counter. He eyed the Beretta on the floor, beyond reach. The man caught his gaze and shook his head. "Uh-uh, tough guy," he sneered. "I'm tellin' my story. Don't want to interrupt me before I'm finished."

"All predators have justifications, rationalizations," Bolan said. He gauged the distance, calculating a strike, knowing that for the best effect he would have to make his move while the other man was talking. Already he was breaking several tactical rules, allowing an enemy to engage him in dialogue, refusing to attack the attacker immediately. But he needed time. If he could resolve this quietly he might still have a chance.

"I ain't no predator, man," the pirate said, frowning. "I'm just me. I fight, that's what I do. There weren't nobody to fight once we got the crew taken care of. Where you been hidin'? I'd have remembered a big boy like you. We're gonna have this out, and maybe for a few minutes at least I won't be bored while they finish their damned game upstairs."

So it did not occur to the pirates, at least not to this one, Bolan thought, that external forces could or would infiltrate the boat. That was good news—it indicated limited thinking. Bolan continued to circle, his knife held before him, wondering when the pirate would make the assault he was sure to initiate once he was finished with his monologue.

"There anybody else in your crew?" The pirate nodded to Bolan's Beretta on the deck. "How many more are there? Where they hidin'? You tell me, man, and maybe I won't cut you up real bad before I kill you. Come on, man, tell a brother how many—"

Bolan struck. He lunged inside the arc of the machete, and drove the point of his knife in a half-circle comma cut toward the man's throat. To his credit, the American pirate was fast. He snapped his head back and brought the spine of the machete up, trying to parry Bolan's knife arm with the only tool available to him. Bolan brought his support arm up across his chest, out of the way, as he snapped the blade of the knife diagonally into the pirate's machete arm. The man howled as his arm was opened up. He stumbled back, dropping the machete and clutching at the terrible wound.

"You son of a—"

Bolan stomped on the man's ankle, snapping it. As the traitorous pirate drew in a breath to scream, Bolan fell on him, driving the butt of the knife into the man's temple. He struck again, then a third time, hammering the pirate insensate before he could make enough noise to expose the Executioner's position.

Bolan scooped up his Beretta, press-checked it and turned back to the fallen American. The big African-American was already beginning to recover, crawling to his knees despite the grievous slash in his forearm. He smiled shakily, one pupil visibly dilated, as he got his legs under him.

"Don't," Bolan warned.

The pirate surged forward.

The Beretta barked a triple-burst of suppressed subsonic rounds. Bolan sidestepped as the pirate plowed into the deck, a strange groan escaping from his throat. He stopped moving and seemed almost to deflate, the death rattle that racked his big frame an almost inhuman sigh. Then the body was very still. Bolan had seen more than enough death to know that the reaper had claimed this wayward American.

He took the body by the legs and dragged it into the nearest cabin. He could not cover the blood on the carpeted deck, so he did not try. Searching the corpse, he found something that worried him—a short-range radio of the type used by hikers, hunters and ATV riders. If he was carrying this it was possible the pirate had been tasked with checking in, or at least radioing back his status when queried. Obviously he'd been hidden somewhere among the officers' quarters, evading Bolan's sweep. It was more than likely he'd been guarding the biohazard canisters.

The numbers of Bolan's combat countdown had fallen to zero. Reloading the Beretta with a fresh magazine, he also checked the Desert Eagle, making sure a round was chambered. With his fist full of 9 mm death and the Desert

Eagle hand cannon by his side, the Executioner took one last look around.

The short-range radio began to crackle in broken English. Whoever was at the other end was asking for the pirate to check in.

Bolan started to run.

3

Tranh Khong held his Kalashnikov close to his bare chest, cradling it one-handed against his wiry frame as he breathed in the smell of fear. In his hand he clutched a dog-eared sheet of paper, printed from one of the machines in the bridge of the *Duyfken Ster.* He ran down the list with his eyes, his lips moving over missing and stained teeth, as he matched the two names to those listed on the screen of the wireless phone he also held in that hand. He then flipped the phone shut and stuck it in his pocket, pausing to adjust the heavy brown leather pouch slung haphazardly through the belt loops of his cutoff jeans. The device inside was as necessary, if not more so, than his phone or all the radio equipment aboard. Even so, it still galled him to have to haul it around.

"They are here," he said in English, as much to worry the cowering captives as because it was the closest thing his band of thugs had to a common language. Forgetting his minor irritations, he looked out over the men, women and children sitting on the floor of the lounge. Most of them had their heads in their hands as they knelt or sat cross-legged amidst the colorful slot machines and other gambling tables. Tranh smiled a gap-toothed smile, jerking his chin toward a female couple near the middle of the multilevel lounge. Two of his crew hurried to obey, the worn French MAT-49 submachine guns in their hands no less deadly for their age.

They were a motley collection, Tranh and his pirates. The majority were Javanese, castoffs from the coastal scum that Tranh found easily enough when he made port and recruited in the local dives. One was even American, a man named Jones, whom Tranh used for his most brutal tasks. A couple were Indonesians of Chinese descent, and one was Vietnamese like Tranh. They wore ill-fitting and cut-down clothing, a mixture of military surplus fatigues—like the sleeveless camouflage BDU jacket Tranh wore open over his jutting ribs—shorts, combat boots or sandals, and whatever civilian clothing they liberated in raids. Thrust in their belts or worn in mismatched holsters and web gear were the weapons they had accumulated—everything from Kalashnikovs like Tranh's, to modern and even antique handguns. They had a few M-16s, and a Soviet-made rocket-propelled grenade launcher that, Tranh had been told, had once been the war trophy of Afghani *mujahideen*.

All but one of his group were men. The woman among them, known only as Merpati, was as vicious a creature as Tranh had ever encountered. It would be wrong to say Tranh's men passed her around. It was more accurate to say that Merpati chose to go from berth to berth among them, doling out her favors at her whim, drawing her knife on those who offended her or who would not stomach refusal on those rare occasions she offered it. Tranh himself had put mutilated corpses overboard on two occasions, after Merpati's ill humor claimed the would-be lover of the moment.

The pirates' backgrounds could not have been more diverse, really, but they had things in common. They were, to a man, killers and cutthroats, criminals wanted for all manner of brutal, miserable crimes. Theirs was almost a club, a gang, their predatory lifestyles joining them in a kinship none of them would have been able to express had they been fully aware of it. Tranh himself was only dimly capable of defining it within his head. It did not matter, ultimately. Only profit, only their continued success, mattered to Tranh. He had taken on this job as much for long-term goals of survival as for the short-term gain of the pay the Russian had offered him. One fed the other. One *was* the other. It was enough.

Adnan bin Noor chattered something in Malaysian, which Tranh understood well enough. Noor held one of the small walkie-talkies they'd liberated from a small fishing trawler raided months ago. Noor was not happy, and when Tranh heard what he had to say, Tranh was not happy, either.

Jones was not answering.

Tranh had picked Jones for the critical task of guarding the Russian's tanks because he knew the man was not easily distracted. Jones lived to kill and seemed to take no pleasure in the other distractions Tranh's crew pursued. He did not drink, to Tranh's knowledge, and he never took his pleasure with those few women they encountered when raiding vessels.

If Jones was not at his post and not answering his radio, something was probably wrong. And that was bad, for if Tranh was to collect the ransom for the hostages and then fulfill the Russian's demands in order to get the remaining half of the payment promised, he would have to adhere to the Russian's timetable.

It was exactly the wrong time for one of the few men on whom Tranh was depending to stop being where he was supposed to be, to stop answering when he was called.

Tranh snatched the radio from Noor. "Jones!" he said. "Jones! Answer!"

He heard nothing but static.

Tranh began barking orders. The hostages sensed the sudden tension in his words and manner, and began to cower, whimper and cry even more. Tranh was tempted to have a few of them pistol-whipped, but he didn't have time.

He instructed several of his men to take up arms and head to the deck below. They would find Jones and find out what had happened, what had gone wrong. Tranh, in the meantime, would do the only thing he could, and that was stick to the schedule the Russian had given him. He searched the room again for those he had just located.

"You," he said, moving to stand over two of the captives. One was a blond woman in her forties, the other a brunette female in her twenties. They looked enough alike to be mother and daughter, which in fact they were. According to the pictures and names sent to him by the Russian, their presence confirmed by the passenger manifest, the two were Mrs. Pamela McAfferty and her daughter, Patricia, wife and daughter to Jim McAfferty. McAfferty was, Tranh had been told by the Russian, a "hawk," whatever that meant, a congressman in the American state of New York.

Tranh did not know or care what the significance of any of that might be; he did not follow politics in any nation, much less the United States. He knew all that was required for his task. The woman and her daughter were family to a government official in the United States, and thus their presence would ensure that the Russian's message was not ignored. They would also, hopefully, prompt the rich Westerners to pay the ransom he had demanded. The Russian had warned him the ransom was a ruse, a means of lulling their victims into thinking this was a typical hijacking, and that meant there might not be time to have it paid. That was all right. The Russian would compensate Tranh for any losses in that quarter, and so far he had made it clear that he had the money to do so.

It was really that simple. Tranh despised complications and sought to keep things as simple as possible, always.

"We weren't doing anything, I swear!" The mother looked up at Tranh with tears in her eyes. "Please don't hurt us! We'll do what you say!"

"Mom," the younger woman spoke. "Stop."

"Yes," Tranh said, smiling. "Do what the girl says. Your husband. Her father. Jim McAfferty, the government man." It was not a question, and Tranh's mediocre English did not diminish the menace in his words. "Yes?"

The mother began sobbing. It was the girl who looked Tranh in the eye, impressing the pirate captain with her mettle. "Yes, my father is Jim McAfferty. You know that already or you wouldn't have asked."

Tranh laughed, crumpled the printout of the ship's manifest and tossed it casually aside. "Yes," he said. "Yes, you right. Wu!"

The Chinese pirate known as Wu, one of the two with a submachine gun trained on the women, stepped forward. He knew his role. Wu had been educated in the West and was fluent in English. He would therefore deliver the written message the Russian had prepared. Wu was easily among the more intelligent members of Tranh's crew, and could be trusted to do this properly. The Russian had demanded Tranh's assurances on this, as it was a very important component of the operation. Tranh had no fear of making such guarantees. He had heard Wu drone on in English often enough, about matters that were well above his head. Tranh knew himself just well enough to know that he was not smart. He was cunning. He was ruthless. He was clever. But he had never considered "smart" to be one of his qualities. He did not care, either, so long as he was able to lead his crew and make money.

Of course, also unlike Wu, he was not a child molester

and a murderer who had been forced to flee more than one small nation when his habits became known. But such were the paths taken by the floating debris of the world's people before they came to the docks that Tranh frequented in his recruiting.

Tranh sometimes wondered, when he grew introspective like this, if perhaps he was not more intelligent than he gave himself credit for. As always, he dismissed these thoughts before they could weigh him down.

There was work to be done, money to be made.

He spoke a few words of command to Noor, who nodded. The pirate stepped over several mewling hostages and, from behind one of the circular bars dominating the colorful, decadently appointed lounge, extracted several pieces of satellite video broadcast equipment. With practiced ease—Noor had been some sort of electronics technician before murdering his lover's lover, if Tranh remembered rightly—he began to assemble and connect the equipment. First he ran the power cables. Then he assembled the small portable reflective dish, positioning it at the end of the lounge at the open entrance to the rear balcony. Finally he positioned the camera and switched it on, motioning for Wu to drag a chair from one of the gambling tables. The Chinese pirate did so, taking up his seat. From his pocket he produced the folded and refolded sheets of paper that contained the Russian's message.

Tranh pulled back the bolt on his Kalashnikov just far enough to determine that a round was chambered. The hostages would be paralyzed with fear once they heard the message. He could not have any heroes making attempts against him before he was ready.

There would be one or two among the crowd who, understanding the full meaning of the Russian's transmitted message, would realize there was nothing to lose and perhaps everything to gain by resisting.

Tranh would show them that there were still losses he could inflict. He would shoot for the legs and then torture any who resisted. It would help him pass the time until the Russian's damnable operation was completed and he could collect his pay.

Noor muttered something, which Tranh took to mean that they were finally ready. He motioned to Wu with his Kalashnikov. The Chinese man cleared his throat and looked into the camera lens, waiting for the light that told him the broadcast had begun. Then he spoke, his English almost without accent, his voice clear, as he read ponderously from the Russian's sheaf of papers.

"Attention, dogs of the West," Wu said, his lack of inflection a curious contrast to the words the Russian had written in English. "For too long, the imperialist West has lorded its wealth and its power over the rest of the world. For too long, arrogant Western nations and their lapdog allies have been free to send their troops around the globe, bombing and attacking and killing whomever they pleased. For too long, the world's smaller nations have lacked the ability to fight back.

"This lack ends today. Included in this transmission…" Wu paused, as was indicated on his notes, looking up at Tranh. Tranh nodded and removed the special transceiver the Russian had given him from the leather pouch at his belt. He pressed a button on the device. The LEDs began to blink green, though the Cyrillic labeling on them meant nothing to Tranh. Finally, the device's lights winked out, one by one. Tranh nodded again to Wu.

"Included in this transmission," Wu began again, "is coded data. Those who need to decipher it will know how. Using this information you may contact your benefactor—"

Wu stumbled a little over the phrasing "—in order to obtain, for a price, the weapon you are to see demonstrated here today."

A murmur went up among the hostages. Tranh was not surprised. He was, in fact, pleased. He wanted that fear caught in the transmission. He had made sure the hostages were in the frame when instructing Noor, through sign language, where to place the camera when the time came. He knew what the Russian wanted. He sympathized, insofar as he was capable of caring about politics. First and always, Tranh cared about enriching himself. If he performed well, the Russian would call on him for other jobs. So far their partnership was new, but had already produced certain benefits, such as the Soviet-era surplus weaponry the Russian had been able to provide.

"This weapon is available to all who wish to purchase it," Wu continued reading. "Provided your goals are to strike a blow at the hated West. In exactly one hour from this transmission, a sample of the weapon will be activated. Video of its effects on those held on this ship will be provided. The volume of the weapon used today is six times the unit of sale. The price and terms for each unit of sale have been included in the coded burst."

Tranh understood, as the Russian had explained to him, the critical timing of the next hour. His men had gas masks and had been made to understand that these would protect them, but this was a lie. The Russian had been very clear that the substance in the canisters, once unleashed, was corrosive. It would eat through masks and the hull of the ship alike, though of course it would eat plastic much more quickly than metal. Two of Tranh's men, with their useless gas masks in place, would stay behind and use the small digital phone cameras, transmitting their digital images to Tranh's own phone. It would be enough for the

Russian's purposes. The men had no idea that they would die before they could leave the ship, of course; their masks would protect them just long enough to let them record the death throes of the passengers before the chemical weapon claimed them, too.

The rest of Tranh's crew would have to be clear of the ship before the canisters detonated. He was relying on Merpati for this; she would bring the speedboat back when her watch, synchronized to Tranh's, reached the appointed time. For now she was moored somewhere out in the darkness.

That darkness worried Tranh. The explosion that had drawn some of his men to the bow of the ship had produced no enemies to shoot. Had there been men to repel, Tranh would feel better. With no one to face, the pirate captain was forced to ponder what the mysterious explosion could mean. He had known there was a chance, however slim, that some law enforcement or military group would stage an attack on the ship in an attempt to save the hostages. He had counted, as had the Russian, on the presence of the American government man's family to discourage such an attempt.

The West was notoriously weak when it came to hostages. As long as they thought there was a chance those held would be released unharmed, they would not use force to resolve the situation. It was one of the things that made the West easy to defeat. For all their superior military might, they were helpless in the face of basic guerilla tactics. Put a gun to a single woman's head and an entire army could be held in check by weak-kneed politicians. Tranh did not pretend to understand this particular failing on the part of such rich, strong countries. He knew only that it worked in his favor.

Wu had finished his recitation and Noor was beginning

to pack up the satellite transmission equipment. The hostages were starting to cry and sob anew as what they had heard began to reach them beyond their fear. Tranh eyed them, finger hovering over the trigger guard of his Kalashnikov, wondering who among them might decide to surge forward.

Then he heard what sounded like gunshots from the lower deck.

Tranh's first thought was that his men had gotten carried way and started firing at each other. Or, he thought, it was possible they had found some passengers hiding somewhere and were eliminating them. When the gunfire continued, however, he became concerned.

Word of the transmission would reach around the world quickly enough, and those whom the Russian sought as customers would seek him out. But the Western powers would be alerted, as well. The Russian had stressed as much; Tranh was well aware that now, with their true plan out in the open, forces might well convene on the ship. An hour's time was supposed to be enough for Tranh to finish his business, make the example and get out, while preventing those who wished to free the hostages from mounting an effective assault.

Merpati was circling the ship in a long, slow patrol of the area, and had detected no approaching vessels. The speedboat had a crude fish-finder electronics package that would, Tranh hoped, alert them to the approach of something large like a submarine. Therefore there was no way they could be taken by surprise unless, somehow, the enemy had risked sending men before the message.

They would have to be on board already.

Tranh turned, Kalashnikov in hand, to face the nearest lounge doorway leading to the companionway to the deck below. Some fleeting forewarning of danger, some dread sensation, made him duck his head and cradle it in his arm.

The deafening blast and sudden burst of brightness sent flashes of white fire dancing through his closed eyes. Tranh was knocked onto his back, the world disappearing in a burst of light and sound.

4

Some pirates streamed past the Executioner as he stood pressed against the bulkhead opposite the corridor where they ran. They had descended from Deck 5, and moved with a haste that could mean only one thing. Time was up. There was no more need for stealth. The pirates knew there was a problem aboard.

Bolan drew the Desert Eagle from its holster with his right hand, filling his left with the Beretta. As one of the pirates approached, Bolan stepped out into the corridor. He leveled both guns at arm's length, drew in a breath, let it out halfway and chose his targets. Then he took up slack on both triggers.

The weapons fired.

The Desert Eagle sounded like the hammer of some angry war god in the enclosed space of the corridor. The pirates were taken completely by surprise as the slugs ripped into them. Bolan made several head shots on the closest targets, his keen marksman's instincts kicking in as he knocked down the enemy like bowling pins. One of the pirates, armed with a sawed-off shotgun, triggered a blast. The pellets went wide and shattered a decorative planter affixed to the bulkhead, blowing the plastic plant to shreds.

The Executioner tracked the man and triggered a single round from the Desert Eagle. The .44 Magnum slug blew a channel between the man's eyes. He crumpled in a twisted heap, dead before he reached the deck.

Two more pirates who had ducked into nearby cabins emerged with Kalashnikovs in their hands. They blazed away down the corridor, their aim wild, fear evident in their faces as the orange muzzle blasts from their rifles lit their faces. Bolan stood his ground, crouching slightly, and pumped a triple burst from the Beretta into one pirate while triggering a .44 Magnum blast into the other.

Sudden silence followed the gunfire.

Bolan quickly assessed his targets visually, verifying that they were dead or out of action. Then he ran back the way he'd come, toward the companionway, holstering the Beretta and charging up to Deck 5 as he unclipped a flash-bang charge from his combat harness.

A pirate with a Kalashnikov somehow saw him and covered his face as Bolan planted one foot against the lounge door. As he shoved the door open, he tossed the primed flash-bang, ducking backward and shielding his ears while squeezing his eyes shut. The grenade burst, a miniature sun filling the lounge with merciless noise.

Bolan waited just long enough for the effects to reach tolerable levels. He stormed the lounge, both guns in his hands, scanning the writhing crowd of hostages and pirates in order to discern hostiles from innocents. The first pirate, the one he'd seen through the door, had crawled off somewhere in the blast. Bolan instead focused on those pirates he could see among the crowd, moving through the lounge with his guns leveled. A pirate clutched at a submachine gun and tried to rise. Bolan shot him. Another attempted to find the door, moving among the screaming, sobbing hostages. Bolan ended his struggles with a single round to the head. The Executioner made several circuits through the large, cluttered lounge space, ending the lives of the pirates before they could harm the hostages. Gunfire echoed and the smell of fired cartridges filled the space, competing with the sounds and smell of fear.

The Executioner knew this world only too well.

Stepping deftly over struggling passengers, who appeared to be recovering from the blast, Bolan found the nearest exit doors, leading forward. He burst through, knowing he could trigger a trap, but knowing, too, that he had no time to spare waiting out his enemies. As he threw himself through, low and fast, the unmistakable burst of Kalashnikov fire ripped through the air above his head. The hollow metallic sound of the AK-pattern receiver was burned indelibly in Bolan's brain, something he would not forget for as long as he lived. From the deck, Bolan brought up both the Desert Eagle and the Beretta, punching snap-fired rounds into the pirate's belly and knocking him down.

Something beeped.

Bolan hurried over, his guns trained on the fallen pirate. The small man, who looked Vietnamese to Bolan's practiced eye, looked up at him, his eyes glazing, as blood pumped from the wounds in his stomach. He made no attempt to reach for the fallen rifle he'd held. On the deck next to him was an electronic device Bolan did not recognize, and an open wireless satellite phone.

"Too…" the pirate said.

Bolan leaned closer, mindful of a sneak attack.

"Too…late…" the pirate whispered.

"What is too late?" Bolan asked urgently. "Who are you?"

"Tranh…" the pirate said, his voice failing. "You… killed…me…" His words turned into a death rattle. "But…you…die."

The pirate stared up in death, eyes empty. The Executioner grabbed the phone. Whatever call the man had made had been disconnected. He tried reestablishing it, but with no luck.

Tranh, Bolan thought. Most likely he *had* been Vietnamese. It was information the Farm might need. Who had he called? Allies nearby? There was no way to know. But there were more pressing concerns. Bolan scooped up the electronic device. He read over the Russian lettering and examined the blinking indicators.

His eyes widened.

Bolan ran. He checked the hostages visually as he ran back through the lounge, making sure there were no living pirates still moving about. People tried to speak with him, but he ignored them, jumping over those still crouched on the floor, heading for the companionway. He made Deck 4 and found the nearest of the canisters.

The electronic detonator registered a countdown.

Bolan took out his PDA satellite phone and hit the preprogrammed, scrambled contact number for Stony Man Farm. He waited as the call went through. Barbara Price, Stony Man's honey-blond, model-beautiful mission controller, answered almost immediately.

"Barb," Bolan said. "I have a problem, *now.* The canisters I sent pictures of. The detonators on them are counting down. I've got several here. I've got less than fifteen minutes."

"We're analyzing it, Striker," Price said without preamble. "Passing you to Akira now."

Akira Tokaido, one of the Farm's expert computer hackers, came on the line. "I have traced the schematics of the device based on the pictures," he told Bolan. "It's a Soviet-era signal receiver and detonator package containing a small but powerful Russian plastic explosive."

"The canisters?" Bolan asked. "What's in them?"

"No time," Akira said. "But trust me, Striker, you don't want them exploding."

"Evacuation?"

"There are three hundred passengers and crew on that ship." Barbara Price's voice cut in again. "We can't get them out in time. We could airlift a few, but not nearly enough."

"Options?

"Each device can be deactivated separately. But you've got to hurry," Akira said. "Each device contains four screws on the side panel. Unscrew those and expose the internal wiring. There are blue, brown and red wires. Cut the blue wire in each detonator. That's it."

"Tamper safeguards?"

"None," Akira said. "It's designed to be simple."

Bolan was already removing the folding multitool he carried in his combat harness. He snapped open the screwdriver bit and began unscrewing the panel on the detonator. When the wires were visible, he cut the blue one.

The countdown stopped. The detonator's LEDs winked out.

The soldier had no time to celebrate his victory. He moved from canister to canister and then from cabin to cabin, finding and neutralizing the detonators as he went. He could not afford to miss any. The numbers fell as he worked furiously, hoping that there were no other pirates loose aboard to make trouble while he undid this horrific work. When he reached the final canister in the last officer's cabin, he saw the readout on the device.

He was not going to make it.

The cabin had a porthole. Bolan ripped the Desert Eagle from its holster and pumped several rounds through the heavy glass. Then he knelt, letting the Desert Eagle rest on the floor. He picked up the canister, adrenaline and desperation lending strength to his movements. He heaved the heavy steel tank, detonator and all, out the porthole, past the broken shards of glass. He waited to hear it hit the sea.

It exploded.

The Executioner could feel the vibrations through the deck and against the hull. He backed away, slowly, knowing that it would do no good if the sea had not neutralized or contained the canister's deadly contents. When he was racked with no ill effects, he took out his PDA once more and dialed the Farm.

"It's done," Bolan said. "One of the tanks exploded in the water after I threw it overboard. What can you tell me?"

"You should be okay, Striker," Barbara Price's voice responded, relief only too evident in her tone. "Bear and Akira have a full workup on what we're dealing with, based on the intelligence you forwarded. The Russian lettering sidetracked us briefly, because it was added to the tanks long after they were made. The containers are Saudi in manufacture."

"Tell me," Bolan said simply. He was making his way to Deck 5 once more, as he listened.

"The substance is a concentrated acid developed by the Saudis," Price informed him. "U.S. Intelligence knew about it maybe twelve years ago. As far as we knew the Saudis themselves quashed it because they were worried it was too powerful."

"What does it do?"

"It's bad, Striker," Price said. "A few drops of it poured onto the ground, exposed to the air, creates a toxic cloud that acts like nerve gas. It's corrosive, too, so it eats through protective seals and right through gas masks."

"When blown up?"

"When explosives are used on it, it becomes much more volatile," Price confirmed. "If those canisters had blown aboard ship, the toxic cloud produced would have killed everyone on board, and anyone in an open boat within a few hundred yards of the ship, depending on the wind."

"Deadly," Bolan said.

"That's why the Saudis tried to put the genie back in the bottle," Price said. "They executed the scientist who created it, in fact. That was largely believed to be for show. But they were serious about containing it, making sure it didn't leave the country."

"Seems the Saudis didn't want to become known as sponsors to the world's terror organizations with this new weapon," Aaron "The Bear" Kurtzman, head of the Stony Man cybernetics team, put in. "You know how tenuous their relationship with us has always been."

"Exactly," Barbara Price confirmed. "U.S. Intelligence sources call it Theta-Seven, though none of our people are quite sure what the Saudi designation was, or is. Last we knew the existing supply had all been destroyed. At least, that's what the Saudis told U.S. government officials through channels, at the time."

"Obviously some slipped through the cracks," Bolan said, stopping as he entered the Deck 5 lounge. The passengers were shaken but appeared to be overcoming the effects of the explosion. The notion that perhaps their long nightmare was ending finally seemed to be dawning on them, at least in a few cases.

"The pirates are neutralized," Bolan said. "What about the tank in the water?"

"Don't eat the fish that'll be floating around the boat," Kurtzman said darkly, "but the acid is heavier than water. It would have descended. The hull might be scarred a little, or even damaged, based on the power of the explosive charge. But you're not in danger of breathing any nerve gas clouds."

"All right," Bolan said. "Get the authorities in on this. We need people aboard this ship. The cruise line will need to assign personnel. I don't know how many of the crew are dead, but it's probably a lot. We'll need medical teams, too. I don't know how many of these people were brutalized. And the ship will have to be searched from top to bottom. There could be some pirates or passengers hiding until this blows over."

"We're going through the appropriate channels," Price told him. "You should have more support on site than you can handle shortly."

"Good," Bolan said. "Striker out."

The Executioner moved among the hostages, doing what he could to reassure them. Several of them thought the big black-clad warrior was another of the pirates, at first, despite what he'd done to those holding them. Bolan saw to it that some of the more responsible among the adults, those who admitted to having previous experience with firearms, were given weapons taken from the pirates. A few were officers from among the ship's crew, Bolan was grateful to see.

"Excuse me, sir?" a young woman's voice called to him. Bolan turned to see someone he recognized from the briefing Stony Man had sent him electronically. It was Congressman Jim McAfferty's daughter. The young woman's mother was close by, looking shell-shocked.

"Yes?" he asked.

"Are you…are you with the government?"

"I'm here to see to it everyone gets home safely," Bolan told her.

"Yes, we're grateful for that, sir," the young woman said. "Only… Could you come take a look at the observation deck? There's a motorboat out there."

Bolan looked to the entrance to the Deck 5 observation

area, beyond the lounge. He ran past the ornate doors, and felt the salty night air on his face as he made for the railing.

The speedboat was just coming around the rear of the cruise ship.

Bolan removed the small monocular from his combat harness and activated the light-enhancing mode. He trained the little device on the speedboat. There was a woman aboard, piloting the good-sized craft as it made a tight arc around the rear of the much larger vessel. Bolan could hear the distant motorboat engine lose speed and then idle as the speedboat began to drift lazily.

The woman leaned down to get something from inside the boat.

Bolan's combat sense told him something was very, very wrong. He ran from the railing, stopping just inside the lounge, scanning the bodies. He found what he was looking for—a Kalashnikov on the deck, near a dead pirate. Bolan snapped it up and ran back for the observation deck. He risked the precious moment it took to peer through the monocular once more.

The woman in the speedboat was lining up on his position with a rocket-propelled grenade launcher.

Bolan, as accomplished a sniper as ever the United States military and years of private warfare could produce, snapped the Kalashnikov to his shoulder. Neither a particularly accurate nor particularly long-range weapon, it was all he had, and it would have to do. Bolan brought the sights on target, prayed they were reasonably true and pulled the trigger.

The rifle shot low, but Bolan's aim was good. The steel-cased round punched a hole through the woman's throat, snapping her head back. The rocket-propelled grenade fired into the air, making a lazy arc before it landed in the sea some distance away. Bolan heard no explosion.

The Executioner lowered his weapon.

Behind him, in the lounge, life would go on.

Somewhere in the dark, as waves lapped at the speedboat's hull, death had claimed another predator.

5

The heat of central Java hit Bolan anew as he stepped out of the taxi, which, though not air-conditioned, had at least offered some shade. In deference to the climate, the soldier wore khaki cargo pants and light desert-tan boots, with a flowing tunic of local design. He would wear his weapons, once acquired, under the tunic. For the moment, he was unarmed, a fact of which he was keenly aware. Frequently during entry into foreign nations, he was forced to strip down to the bare essentials. As often as it happened, he did not like it, and never would. It was simply a necessary evil.

All around Bolan the bustling city of Semarang, a curious collection of traditional and modern, pulsed with life. The streets were not as congested as those of other Indonesian and South Asian cities he'd visited, but a stream of small cars, buses, motorbikes and bicycles passed by him nonetheless. From what he had seen of Semarang so far, Bolan had been impressed with the amount of greenery in place, and with the city's general state of repair. While an industrial city, Semarang was also a business hub and popular tourist destination, boasting many temples and museums worth visiting. So said the travel literature Aaron Kurtzman had condensed and transmitted to Bolan's PDA, along with tactical briefings concerning the city's layout and major landmarks.

In the thirty-six hours that had passed since the liberation of the *Duyfken Ster,* the Farm's computer team had sleuthed out volumes of information, including a complete analysis of the electronic device Bolan had recovered from the dead pirate. Brognola had conferred with the Farm and called Bolan himself the previous evening, letting him know that local resources were being activated and would be available come morning.

"We've uncovered a lot," the big Fed had told him, sounding as worried as ever, "but what we now know points to further complications."

"Shoot," Bolan said.

"The transmitter you received, and the detonators used to detonate the Theta-Seven, were surplus Russian military hardware," Brognola informed him. "By itself, that doesn't narrow things down much. But the transmitter was something more than just a remote trigger. It's a sophisticated piece of communications technology that the Soviets once issued to naval officers. The theory was that if regular communications were broken off, for whatever reason, the Soviets' own satellite network—not unlike the GPS network—could be used to keep their ships and planes in contact with the Kremlin. It was a world-war scenario, technology created during the height of the Cold War."

"How does that help us?" Bolan asked.

"The transmitters were issued to specific officers with specific coded carrier signal signatures," Brognola said, sounding as if he were quoting the information from a file. "After the Soviet Union collapsed and the Russian armed forces started having financial problems maintaining their equipment, there were a lot of desertions, particularly among the navy. A lot of people disappeared, taking these transmitters with them. They've resurfaced on the black market worldwide, are sold for cash, and they do still transmit globally. The satellite network is largely intact, though our people tell us they'll start to fail over the next couple of decades."

"So the transmitter was used to communicate with others still accessing that network?" Bolan asked.

"Right," Brognola said. "We know that al Qaeda, for one, uses the network from time to time, a legacy of the Soviet conflict in Afghanistan. We know the Chinese can access it. And there are a half a dozen well-financed terror groups who can access it, as well as a few of our allies. The Israelis and the Germans, for example."

"That doesn't narrow down the potential sales base, then," Bolan said. The Farm had sent him a condensed video file of the transmission sent by the pirates just before Bolan had hit them. It was clear that the taking of the cruise ship had been a demonstration, a means of showing terrorists worldwide just what Theta-Seven could do. Had they been able to narrow down the list of potential buyers, they might have a means of backtracking the acid to its source.

"It doesn't," Brognola said, "but as I just said, the transmitters were issued to specific personnel. The Russians still have the list of codes and the officers to whom they were assigned. One of our contacts within the Russian military has come through for us. The code in question was assigned to an officer who has deserted, and as far as we know, the device has not been sold on the open market. There is a very good chance he is the source of the Theta-Seven, the sponsor of the pirate attack."

"Who is it?"

"A Captain Vadim Olminsk," Brognola said. "He fits the profile, as near as we can tell, though the Russians have lost most of his other records. We did manage to track down several assets he holds, including property in Semarang. And he has several private ships. More specifically, a company he owns has a controlling interest in a small fleet of freighters."

"The *Duyfken Ster* made port in Semarang before it was attacked," Bolan said.

"Exactly," Brognola said. "Which puts Olminsk local. As it turns out, he has considerable holdings related to import and export. Exactly the sort of thing he'd be moving if he was engaging in some piracy of his own, or coordinating with a pirate group or groups and fencing for them."

"Looks like I hunt in Semarang, then."

"I'm arranging for local support for you now. The intelligence network in Java is sketchy. They don't have a lot of power. But they do have men and women who are willing to work with us. They're almost second-class citizens in their own regime, but they know the local landscape and they'll be able to help. Up to a point."

"Understood. You mentioned further complications," Bolan said.

"There are two. The first is that we can't get a chemical sample from the canisters we've recovered. The detonators were easily enough neutralized, as you well know. But each canister has an internal tamper switch wired directly to it, with a chemical-mechanical trigger. It's one way. Once it's switched on, any attempt to extract the contents will trigger a small explosion—enough to volatilize the acid."

"So you'll have to destroy the canisters and you can't analyze what's inside."

"Exactly," Brognola said. "Which means we're no closer to knowing if there's some way to counter it, to neutralize it, or to treat someone who has been exposed. The good news is that it doesn't look like these triggers would *necessarily* be activated on every canister. It wouldn't make sense for the Saudis to put the stuff in there with no way to deactivate the canisters. It looks like a field fail-safe. We think, at this point, that Olminsk himself would have done it in deploying the devices."

"So I might yet come across one we can open."

"You might. That's not the full extent of the bad news, though," Brognola continued, sounding grave. "We've made some inquiries. The Saudis are already on the trail of the Theta-Seven. From what we can tell they've got their elite security in on this."

"Not good," Bolan admitted.

"No," Brognola said. "So watch yourself, Striker."

"Always. Any luck with the contact data in the burst transmission?"

"Cut-outs, message services and package drops, again all in Semarang. We'll have our people on them, but Olminsk would know that customers and law enforcement alike could interpret his transmission, so he'll be ready for that. Chances are we won't get anything from them. But we have them under surveillance nonetheless."

"All right. Keep me informed," Bolan said.

"Will do, Striker," Brognola had concluded the call. "Good hunting."

Now, on the streets of downtown Semarang, Bolan chose a direction and began walking. He did his best to look as if he belonged. It was, he knew, a losing battle. He would have looked out of place in Indonesia as a six-foot Westerner anyway, but Semarang also boasted a large ethnically Chinese population. In neither case was Bolan likely to pass for a local. He simply did as always in such places, walking confidently as if he had somewhere specific to be.

He had, however, no destination. His instructions had been to take a taxi from his hotel to downtown Semarang and wait to be acquired by the Farm's local asset, an informant and covert operative. Bolan had not been given a name or a photograph and had not expected either. If he was approached by someone pretending to be the contact at this early stage in the game, chances were that the entire operation was blown and it was going to turn into a bloodbath fast.

The Executioner fully intended for that bloodbath to occur, of course, once the appropriate targets had been identified, but he could not afford for it to come too soon or to catch innocents in the line of fire. That was the balancing act he always made when engaged in an operation, the uncompromising principle by which he operated.

Bolan made his way along the outskirts of the town square. The busy shopping center, also host to various festivals and public performances, thrummed with activity. Food vendors and souvenir hawkers ran portable and semi-portable stalls and carts. Everything from office supplies to home furnishings and clothing was offered there. He took a moment to enjoy the atmosphere, knowing that this calm before the coming battlestorm could not last.

The taxi that pulled to the curb just ahead of him had a whistling fan belt that sounded like it was not long for this world. The driver got out and walked away. Bolan's keen eyes caught the brown-skinned hand beckoning to him through the open window. Checking side to side and glancing behind him to confirm no ambush was in the offing, Bolan stepped forward. A squeal of rusty hinges cut through the traffic noise as the man in the backseat pushed open the door from within.

"Come, come," he said, still beckoning to Bolan. "There is not much time."

Bolan took a seat. The man next to him wore a loose-fitting red-and-tan-patterned shirt of traditional Indonesian fabric, a black felt hat that reminded Bolan of a fez and baggy three-quarter-length shorts of beige fabric. He wore sandals on his feet, one of which was prominently displayed as he sat with one leg crossed over his lap. In his left hand, held low and across his stomach, was a small Beretta Jetfire pocket automatic.

"I am Pramana Suharto," he said in slightly accented English, offering his right hand and grinning through bright white teeth. "Please forgive me for this mixed message." He gestured with the gun, though the muzzle never strayed from the general direction of Bolan's abdomen. "I must confirm that you are whom you are supposed to be."

"You picked *me* up," Bolan said.

"That is true." Suharto shrugged, the gesture somehow odd for his rounded shoulders and Javanese manner. "But one large, dark-haired American looks much like any other."

"Black flag," Bolan said, using the code phrase Brognola had provided.

"Indeed." Suharto laughed. He hid the little handgun somewhere under his shirt. "As you know, I was given no spy-sounding words to say in response."

"No," Bolan said. "I'm Matt Cooper."

"I will live, Mr. Cooper," Suharto said. His face fell. "At least for the moment."

"You don't sound too happy."

"In truth, I am not," Suharto said. "Neither is my government, nor the Indonesian Intelligence Agency. You are seen as a...meddling influence."

"Am I?"

"Please understand," Suharto said. "I hold no opinions one way or another, in most respects. Though I do worry that your influence here will destabilize an already volatile situation."

"How so?"

"Mr. Cooper, how do I put this delicately? Your nation

tends to shoot first and ask questions later, if at all. You are seen as, what is the word, *mavericks*. You do not respect the wishes of the international community. You pressure small nations to let you interfere, and they invariably capitulate. Such is the situation here. I have been told I must assist you. I have been told we must allow you to operate here in this country, taking over an investigation into which by rights your country should have no authority. This is an Indonesian problem that should be solved by Indonesians, not by American gunfighters."

"Is that what you think I am?" Bolan asked.

"Are you not?"

"You may have a point," Bolan conceded. "And I don't pretend to agree with all the political decisions of my country. But I'm here to do a job. Specifically, I'm here to make sure a lot of people who don't deserve to die, don't— and that those who are guilty pay."

"You see?" Suharto said. "That is the attitude to which I refer. That is why I fear."

"I won't lie to you," Bolan told him. "This could get bloody. We're dealing with dangerous people who understand only superior force. They don't understand reason. They don't respond to bargaining. They don't possess pity, or mercy. They're animals, of a sort. They're predators who take what they want and don't care who gets hurt. It's my job to fight them. I've been doing it for a long time, now."

"I understand," Suharto said.

"Now," Bolan said, "I'm going to ask for your help. Let's forget about the machinations of our governments for a minute. Politics are irrelevant. This is an agreement between you and me. I'm asking for your help because I need local assistance to do this job. I promise you that my goal is to preserve innocent life while bringing the guilty to justice. If you can accept that, I'd like you to agree to help me. But only if *you* want to. I won't force you to, no matter what my government or your superiors have to say about it."

Suharto considered that for a moment. "Thank you, Mr. Cooper. That is a level of respect I had not expected." He thought about it for a moment more. "Yes," he said deliberately, "I will. I will help you. Because it is the right thing to do."

"All right, then," Bolan said. He held out his hand. "This is an agreement between us, not our governments."

Suharto shook the offered hand, his grip strong. "Agreed."

Turning to business, the Indonesian produced a small notebook from a pocket of his shorts. "Take this. It contains the complete list of assets under investigation by the Saudi security forces."

"Any explanation why?" Bolan asked.

"In some cases the locations are linked to freight companies and other business concerns ultimately traceable to Olminsk," Suharto said. "His is an extensive network of financial ties, given the amount of goods he moves. While much of it is done completely untraceably, some is still linked to him—accounts he holds, bank transactions he has made. In other cases we believe the Saudis have been conducting direct surveillance."

"You have someone on the inside with the Saudis?"

Suharto shrugged.

"So they've known about the problem for a while," Bolan pressed.

"Of course. They would have been the first to know that the chemical had gone missing."

"Let's not reinvent any wheels, then," Bolan said. "Give me the list in order of priority."

"We travel first to the Old City," Suharto nodded. "There is a small office near Gereja Blenduk, one of the front companies for Olminsk's import/export business."

"Gereja Blenduk?"

"Ah, a most delightful structure. The oldest Christian church in central Java. Built by the Dutch in the mid-seventeen hundreds, I am told. You will be delighted by the architecture in the old city. Semarang is a city of rich cultural heritage."

"I'm afraid I won't have much time to see the sights."

"Regrettable." Suharto nodded.

"After this office?"

"We are scheduled to meet with a contact at the rail station," Suharto said. "An informant loosely tied to our organization. He will bring me an update on the Saudi security forces' activities. His information may trump the tentative list I have put together."

"If it doesn't?"

"Then," Suharto said thoughtfully, "we will visit a warehouse not far from the harbor. It is in the Terboyo industrial estate, the largest in the city. Beyond that there is only…it is somewhat amusing…the city zoo."

"The zoo?" Bolan looked skeptical.

"Tinjomoyo Zoo, yes," Suharto said, almost embarrassed. "Our local resources uncovered the link. It is not one the Saudis considered important."

"Why would they?" Bolan asked.

"It seems that among the cargos taken by Olminsk, or those working with him—we believe a coalition of multiple pirate crews reports to him in exchange for his financial compensation and logistical support for the stolen freight—there were several species of exotic animals. Many were birds. A few mammals, more reptiles. Creatures with value, it would seem. Many have turned up in the zoo. We believe the head of acquisitions there, Santoso Atunarang, is in contact with Olminsk and might be able to provide us with some information. He is low priority and may not know anything. We have been careful not to let on what we suspect. He will, as you say, keep."

"Then let's roll on the office," Bolan said. "You have a package for me?"

"Care of your people, yes." Suharto nodded. "Very… heavy."

"You looked inside?"

"Of course. I was most jealous." The Indonesian patted his shirt, over the little pistol. "It puts my little gun to shame." Suharto waved to the driver to return.

Bolan said nothing. He watched the streets of Semarang as they drove, cataloging the sights and sounds, memorizing as much as he could. Such information about the combat environment could be invaluable if he found himself running and gunning on the streets of Semarang. He hoped to avoid such a public display, if possible. He could not afford to endanger innocents, but beyond that, Brognola would have considerable trouble with the State Department if Bolan chewed up the international landscape too badly. It had happened before. While he would always do what needed to be done, the Executioner tried not to make the big Fed's perpetual heartburn any worse than it already was.

The taxi—which Bolan knew was not a taxi at all, but a disguised vehicle driven by one of Suharto's men—brought them to a narrow alley between two commercial buildings, a block away from the office location Suharto intended to raid. The Indonesian beckoned to Bolan as he exited the vehicle.

"In the boot," he said, indicating the car's trunk. Bolan looked around to make sure they were not immediately visible to anyone. He reached into the trunk, which Suharto popped open with a key, and removed the heavy duffel bag inside. Unzipping the bag, he found the supplies the Farm had provided for him.

Bolan's custom leather shoulder holster was there, complete with its suppressed Beretta 93-R machine pistol with loaded spare magazines in the offside pouches. His sheath and belt pouches for the Desert Eagle and its magazines were also there, as was his green canvas war bag with its various deadly accessories. Kissinger had included two knives, as well: a tactical folding knife and a large spear-point combat knife. The larger knife had an inside-the-waistband Kydex sheath. It was not until Bolan finished digging through these and shrugging into the shoulder holster that Bolan realized just how the Farm's weapon-smith had outdone himself.

Bolan hefted the primary weapon provided to him for the Semarang operation. The compact, space-age submachine gun looked like something out of a science-fiction movie. The advanced prototype, tuned by Kissinger and fitted with a red-dot sight, laser and weapon-light system mounted to the top rail, had a folding stock and vertical foregrip integrated in an extremely lightweight, ergonomic package. The .45-caliber weapon had fully automatic, two-round burst and semi-auto fire control fed from modified 30-round Glock magazines. The weapon included a shoulder strap that connected to grommets on Bolan's shoulder harness, allowing him to sling it muzzle-down under his right arm. He found spare loaded Glock magazines in his war bag.

"Shall we?" Suharto nodded in the direction of the office, which was around the corner and down the street from the alley.

"Let's," Bolan said. He checked the fit of the Vector under his arm, making sure he could get to it under his tunic.

"You are ready for a war," Suharto said.

"Always," Bolan nodded.

6

"Tovarisch Imports," Suharto read the sign aloud as he and Bolan approached the front of the small office building. Around them, the Dutch architecture of the Old City lent a charm to Semarang that was obvious to even the most busy or distracted of travelers. Even Bolan, focused on the task at hand, could acknowledge the idiosyncratic beauty of this exotic, dynamic city. He glanced up and down the street as they approached the front of the structure. He saw no obvious hostiles, nor any hidden surveillance, but knew he could never be certain.

"Let's introduce ourselves," Bolan said.

"How do you, as they say, wish to play it?" Suharto asked.

"Straight in and straight up," Bolan said grimly. "Let's see if anything shakes loose."

"As you wish," Suharto said. He had a sawed-off double-barreled shotgun, an ancient weapon that was at least much more backup than his little pistol. He had concealed it under his voluminous shirt with ease. Now he hitched at it, obviously nervous. It was the sort of tic that often gave away those concealing unfamiliar weapons.

"Easy," Bolan warned. "Just keep your head down and move forward. You'll be fine."

"My expertise is largely intelligence," Suharto admitted. "I have not been called on for much in the way of bloody battle."

"Don't worry," Bolan said. "I have."

"I do not doubt it." Suharto grinned nervously.

Bolan stepped through the doorway to Tovarisch Imports, squinting and scanning the dimly lit room after leaving the bright sunshine of the hot Indonesian morning. The close, almost claustrophobic office was cluttered with cardboard boxes and littered with paper wrappers. It smelled of stale food and, faintly, rotting garbage. Behind the gouged and chipped wooden desk in the center of the office sat a large man, staring at the flat-screen monitor of a desktop computer. He looked up, his features creased in irritation, as they entered.

Bolan took note of the close-cropped blond hair and vaguely Slavic features before the man rose from behind the desk. He was a couple of inches taller than Bolan, a muscular tower of a man wearing oil-stained coveralls. Stony Man Farm had transmitted a grainy picture of Olminsk from what little file data the Russians had. This man was too young and too tall to be the veteran captain.

"This place is private," he said, his deep voice booming in a Russian accent. "You will leave."

"I have a few questions, first," Bolan said calmly. "I'm looking for a Vadim Olminsk. I assume he's your employer. I'd like you to take a message to him."

The flicker in the man's eyes gave him away as he tried and failed to cover his surprise. The lie came easily enough, but too late. "There is no Olminsk here. You are mistaken. Leave now."

"I don't think so," Bolan said. Silently, his right hand moved to the tactical folding knife clipped to his right pocket.

The big Russian was fast. One meaty hand shot out, the man's intent obviously being to grab Bolan by the throat. It was the sort of thing a barroom brawler would do, and it had probably served the big man well often enough. No doubt he usually followed his crushing, choking grip with a flurry of punches to his victim's face.

As the clawlike hand shot for his throat, Bolan ducked and slapped the hand to the side, his right hand simultaneously coming up with the knife in his fist. The knife's angular, viciously serrated, spring-assisted blade snapped open as he brought it up and over, slashing it across the Russian's arm as his support hand slapped the arm into the blade. The Russian howled in fury as he withdrew his bleeding arm reflexively.

Bolan planted his back foot and shot his lead leg out, slamming the sole of his boot into the wooden desk. He shoved it forward, knocking the Russian over, pinning his legs.

Bolan was aware of Suharto drawing back and fumbling for his weapon, but there was no way the Indonesian would get a clear shot in these close quarters. As Bolan moved forward to press his advantage, the Russian twisted, rolling over and gripping his hands around Bolan's waist in a viselike grip. He threw the Executioner bodily across the desk.

The soldier hit the wall, the impact stunning him. He lost his knife and reached for one his guns, knowing he would have only a smallest fraction of an instant before the Russian was on top of him.

"Do not move!" Suharto shouted.

Bolan pushed to his feet to find that both he and the Russian were staring down the twin barrels of Suharto's shotgun.

"You will not fire," the Russian said, blood dripping heavily down his damaged arm. He jerked his head in Bolan's direction. "You will hit him, as well."

"I only just met him, *pak*," Suharto said casually, employing a mocking local term, "and to be honest I do not like him very much. You are welcome to take your chances. I would not put many *rupiah* on my affection for this American."

The Russian hesitated. It was all the time Bolan needed. He had the Desert Eagle out from under his tunic and trained on the back of the Russian's head before the man knew what was happening.

"I have a clear shot," Bolan said.

The Russian growled.

They got him strapped into his own chair using plastic zip-tie cuffs from Bolan's war bag. They also bandaged the Russian's arm.

"Now," Bolan said, standing over the bound man while Suharto and his shotgun guarded the door. "This is the question and answer portion of the program. Where is Olminsk?"

"You think I will tell you?" the Russian scoffed. "I have seen pain, *govnosos.*"

"What did he call you?" Suharto asked.

"Nothing good." Bolan shook his head. "You think you know pain?"

"I have endured it and dealt it," the Russian answered, smiling. He swore again, something Bolan did not recognize.

The Executioner leaned in, making eye contact with his captive. He did not blink as he said, "You have no idea what pain can be. I have seen men, women, even children turned into things that weren't human anymore. I've seen people driven mad by torture. I've ended the lives of those driven to insanity and beyond by the mutilations and violations visited on them. You think you know pain? You know *nothing.*"

The Russian's bravado was false as he tried, shakily, to regain the initiative. "Then torture me, bad man!" he challenged, forcing a laugh. "Show me how much you know! I will laugh and spit as I pass into the next world, knowing you have been denied the information you seek!"

Bolan retrieved his fallen folding knife, cleaned it on the Russian's sleeve and replaced it in his pocket.

He turned back to the prisoner. "I'm not going to torture you," he said. "You don't know anything important enough to justify that."

"Don't I?" the Russian mocked. His courage was returning.

"No," Bolan said. He drew the Desert Eagle, dramatically racking the slide even though there was no need. The live round flew over his shoulder and landed on the floor near Suharto, but the Russian didn't notice. That was because the .44-caliber barrel was pointing at his face as Bolan held it at full extension.

"What are you doing?" the prisoner demanded.

"Killing you," Bolan said flatly. "What does it look like?"

"Wait!" the Russian screamed. "You said you wanted information!"

"You said you wouldn't give it," Bolan replied.

"You cannot simply shoot me!" the Russian shrieked. "I have done nothing wrong!"

"You attacked me," Bolan said from behind the Desert Eagle.

"You…you are trespassers! Unless…are you police?" The Russian offered this almost hopefully, perhaps thinking that policemen would not shoot him in cold blood.

"No, sorry," Bolan said. He pressed the barrel of the Desert Eagle to the man's forehead, moving his support arm in front of his body as if to block the spray of blood that would result.

"Stop!" Suharto said nervously. "Mr. Cooper, I must protest. This man should be taken in for questioning."

"Then you *are* police," the Russian said.

"No, not really," Bolan said. "Do you have any ID in your pocket? There won't be much left at this range."

"I will tell you! I will tell you!" the Russian said. Apparently the cold certainty in Bolan's eyes had been enough for him. His false courage evaporated in the face of Bolan's willingness to take his life.

"Start with your name," Bolan said, the barrel of the Desert Eagle never wavering.

"Grigori!" the Russian said hastily. "Grigori Stechken"

"And tell me, Grigori," Bolan said, his voice low and menacing, "where is Olminsk?"

"We know this place belongs to a company in which he holds controlling interest," Suharto related.

"I do not know, and that is the truth," Grigori said, his head dropping to his chest. "Olminsk is at sea. His exact location is unknown to me."

"The Theta-Seven. Where is it?" Bolan asked.

"The what?"

Bolan placed the vaguely triangular nose of the Desert Eagle against the man's forehead. "The acid. Yellow canisters of deadly acid. Where?"

"I don't know!" Grigori said quickly. "I do not! Olminsk closely guards the location. He said he would have it moved when it was needed, and not before!"

Bolan withdrew the Desert Eagle, dropping the hammer slowly with his thumb, again for dramatic effect. He was counting on this subtle psychological warfare to have more of an effect on the Russian than any amount of outright torture might have. The man was, fundamentally, a coward, who seemingly enjoyed inflicting pain while capable of enduring little of it—psychological or otherwise—himself.

"You are satisfied?" Suharto asked cautiously.

"We won't get much more from him," Bolan nodded. "He doesn't know anything."

Grigori snarled.

"Mr. Cooper," Suharto said quietly, looking out the grimy window in the office door, "we have visitors."

Bolan joined Suharto by the door and glanced outside. Two black Mercedes sedans with tinted windows were rolling into position in front of the office. The men who emerged wore expensive double-breasted suits and head-wraps, and wraparound sunglasses covered their eyes.

"It is the Saudis!" Suharto said. "I recognize one of them. Let me go speak to them. Perhaps I can—"

"Down!" Bolan shouted.

The lead Saudi was removing a chopped MP-5 submachine gun from under his jacket. Bolan grabbed Suharto and pulled him to the floor as a fusillade of 9 mm slugs punched through the flimsy wooden door. In his chair, the Russian squealed and managed to knock himself over, still tied to the rickety seat. Bullets tore up the surface of the cluttered desk and scattered puffs of cardboard and paper around the room.

Bolan rolled, shoving the Desert Eagle back in its holster and deploying his submachine gun. The weapon felt rock-steady and smooth as glass in his hands as he cut loose with a string of two-round bursts. The heavy .45 slugs spat retribution through the splintered door. The lead Saudi was caught in the legs and dropped, screaming, spraying the last of his short magazine into the ground. Bolan aimed carefully through the now-gaping hole in the door and put a mercy round in the man's head.

Then the Executioner was up and pressing his advantage. "Watch him!" he shouted, hoping Suharto would know enough to stay with the prisoner and out of the direct line of fire. He slammed through the remains of the door, using his shoulder, rolling through, out and up, the gun chugging out low-velocity jacketed death.

The Saudis, taken off balance by this sudden shift in battlefield momentum, had scattered. Two had taken cover behind the cars, and Bolan thought there was a very good chance they were bullet-resistant. In a combat crouch, he heel-toed smoothly around the vehicles, his weapon leading the way, never losing his sight picture. The Saudis were almost shocked when he flanked them, turning to bring their weapons—a micro Uzi and another MP-5—to bear on this surprising threat. Bolan tapped a two-round burst into the center of mass of each one, letting the weapon do the work. The .45 bullets dumped the shooters to the ground like poleaxed cattle.

"Back!" Bolan shouted to Suharto. "Watch the back! They're coming around!" While the soldier could not see his foes, there was no other explanation for the sudden disappearance of the other Saudis. They had to be circling to take the building from the rear. He had no idea if there would be an entrance back there or not, but he had to assume as much.

Bolan flattened himself against the wall as one of the Saudis broke cover and fired at him from the back of the structure. The soldier could almost feel the heat of the bullets as they zinged past. He fired one-handed, the internal recoil-reducing system helping him keep his shots on target accurately as he chased the Saudi gunner back into hiding.

Inside, the unmistakable roar of a 12-gauge thundered. Suharto had taken a shot at someone. Bolan hoped he was not too late.

The Executioner took the corner wide to give him a good angle on whoever waited for him. The Saudis had already entered through a rear door. Bolan kicked this aside and, flicking on the submachine gun's weapon light, illuminated the comparative gloom of the office's back room. He caught the first Saudi shooter completely flat-footed, blinking at the sudden burst of white light, squinting with his HK USP pistol off target. Bolan dropped him with a single .45 round to the head.

The second and last Saudi hitter cursed in English and emptied the magazine of his MP-5 in Bolan's general direction. The soldier hit the floor, drawing a bead on the man with his laser unit, stitching his legs out from under the man. The scream was cut off by the blast of Suharto's second barrel. A few errant pellets struck the wall near Bolan's head.

"Suharto!" Bolan shouted. "Hold your fire!"

Past the ringing in his ears from the close-quarters gunfire, Bolan could hear Suharto jacking open his shotgun to reload. The wounded Saudi, meanwhile, was clutching at his wounds, hissing through gritted teeth. Bolan advanced on him, making sure he could see the green light of the laser dancing over his chest. The Saudi made no attempt to reach for the gun he had lost.

"Untie me! Untie me!" Grigori was shouting from his upended chair. "They will kill me to silence me!"

"Probably," Bolan said. He looked to Suharto. "How long before the gunfire draws police?"

"Not long." Suharto shook his head. "We should go, unless you wish to do much explaining."

"You have any pull with the authorities?"

"Not terribly much, I am afraid," Suharto said. "Our organization is largely behind the scenes. We have not much official authority, at least in the eyes of the constabulary."

Bolan nodded. They could spare a few moments, and no more. "Have your man bring the car up," he said.

Suharto took out his phone and activated its walkie-talkie feature. As he did so, Bolan pulled the wounded Saudi into a sitting position.

"You're looking for the acid," he said. It was not a question. The Saudi did not blink and gave no indication that he even understood the statement. Bolan chalked one up to the opposition's credit. They were professionals.

"Cooper," Suharto said. "There is no time."

"There was no need for this," Bolan told the Saudi, waving Suharto off for the moment. "We are working to get the acid out of Olminsk's hands and safely in custody."

The Saudi scowled.

"If you try to stop us, I will take you down, and everyone you send after. Tell your bosses to stay out of my way." Bolan could see that his words were having no effect, but he would not kill the man in cold blood. There would be enough trouble behind the scenes where international relations were concerned. He would gamble that letting this man go to speak with his superiors might have some effect, however mild. At this point there was little to lose by trying the play.

The scrape of the chair alerted Bolan. He looked up just in time to throw himself aside. Grigori had somehow gotten his hands loose—Bolan had a fleeting impression of a pair of scissors on the floor, most likely spilled from the desk in the chaos of the gunfight—and produced a revolver, also likely from within the desk. The first shot took the wounded Saudi in the neck, while the second took him in the head.

Bolan swiveled as he dodged, the Desert Eagle springing into his hand almost unbidden, thumbing back the hammer snapping off a desperation shot that shattered revolver and hand alike. Grigori screamed and held the broken mess that had been his gun hand. He writhed on the floor. His legs were still strapped to the fallen chair.

"Cooper!" Suharto said urgently. "They are coming! I can hear police horns in the distance."

They left the Russian to face the authorities.

7

Captain Vadim Olminsk, late of the Russian navy, stood in the small bridge of the freighter *Milaya Volya,* smoking a cigarette and thinking dark thoughts.

The *Milaya Volya* was nothing compared to the frigate he was once to have commanded. The frigate they had promised him was a mighty *Yastreb*-class. And then the money ran out. The *Milaya Volya* was nothing compared to the outdated gun cruiser he *had* commanded, a Sverdlov whose class Kruschev had condemned as obsolete when the man came to power.

The *Milaya Volya* was itself a conquest, originally manufactured in a Korean shipyard, taken by Olminsk's men not long after his career as an entrepreneur of the seas had begun. It was a flexible ship, able to enter smaller ports, geared with cranes to load and unload freight at those ports lacking such infrastructure. The craft was perfect for Olminsk, perfect for what he was. He was a *pirate,* he forced himself to admit. He found the word ugly and the state of affairs to which his life had come before his embrace of this lifestyle even *more* ugly, but it was what it was.

Those last years in Russia had been hard. The loss of the Cold War and the collapse of the mighty Soviet Union had left the Russian navy in disarray and disrepair, cash poor and bereft of strong leadership.

Lack of money, lack of maintenance, lack of care…

simple, damned neglect and apathy had destroyed what was left of Russia's once proud fleet. The losses had become so great, the dishonor so palpable, the despair so overwhelming, that Olminsk had finally had enough.

He had gathered those sailors in his command who were either loyal or simply willing to try something, anything, to escape the collapse. Then he procured the first of several small raiding vessels and used those to trade up more than once, capturing those ships he thought he could use.

Olminsk and his men had finally settled on the *Milaya Volya* because it had the right balance of size and equipment needed to facilitate the raids that sustained them. From the vessel he could drop motor-powered inflatable rafts used for raiding and boarding, and from the deck of his small freighter he could launch shoulder-held missiles and rocket-propelled grenades. The ship could then carry any cargo and passengers captured—Olminsk had set up crude holding cells in a portion of the hold—and could offload freight at whatever port its captain desired. Years in the navy had taught Olminsk the value of speed and maneuverability, as well as flexibility across a wide variety of unpredictable tactical scenarios.

He had fully expected to scratch out the rest of his life as a miserable pirate, thieving what living he could from those traveling the seas. It was to be an ignominious end to what had started as an auspicious career, only to become a travesty and then a tragedy. As the Soviet Union and the new Russia she had birthed began to collapse around him, Olminsk had resigned himself to death with dishonor.

Strangely, and much to his surprise, he had prospered.

Since embarking on his new career the Russian captain had discovered that there was much wealth to be made, many markets to be tapped, for those willing to work the seas with appropriate ruthlessness. He had done his research, determined the richest and most vulnerable venues for piracy, those shipping lanes where high traffic and low law-enforcement presence made them fertile grounds for his plunder.

He had settled in Semarang. To travel the seas endlessly would be unsupportable. They needed a port from which to operate, however secretly. As their successes grew, they also needed the means to sell, to trade and to fence freight captured, to offload those items that were valuable but not of immediate use to them. Whether it was textiles or food, machine parts or soap, electronics or even mail, whatever could be transported by large, slow ships could be taken by smaller, faster ships bearing armed and ready men. So it was that Olminsk had chosen the port city of Semarang to base his operations. Over the years he had built quite a network.

His pirate allies had likewise come as a surprise, but a welcome one.

Olminsk encountered several different groups of pirates working the area. He had witnessed, at least once, two opposing crews fighting each other, their power launches racing back and forth as crewmen with small arms fired away. The entire exercise struck Olminsk as stupid. Yes, technically, other pirate crews were competition…but if one group of five or ten men could take a ship, what could three or four groups the same size accomplish, especially if coordinated?

It had taken some doing to get the opposing groups to speak with each other at all. He had been forced to kill a few, using his superior tactical knowledge and all of the firepower available to him to muscle over a few of the less cooperative or more paranoid pirate crews. Ultimately, however, he had managed to get three of the other captains to meet with him. There had been some language barriers initially, but he had overcome them, through translators or broken English or even sign language when needed. They had come to terms.

Olminsk would provide them with financial and logistical support. They, in turn, would bring their pillaged and plundered goods directly to him, through his freight and fence network. Everyone benefited. And Olminsk was in a position to grow richest of all. Most of the pirates were fairly stupid, content with simple gestures and ostentatious representations of wealth. Give them liquor, drugs and women, and they were content. They lived for the moment and had no aspirations, no ambitions, save to slake their baser needs through victimizing others. Olminsk understood the type. He had seen it often enough among the dregs of those who found their way into the Russian navy. For that matter, in his time as a naval officer he had seen plenty of men in foreign ports who were just the same.

The exception had been Tranh. While not well-educated by most standards, and certainly as vicious as the maddest of mad dogs, Tranh had an exceptionally able mind. He was cunning, quick and relatively capable of controlling himself when he thought it necessary. He was both an effective manager of the criminals working with him, and an able field operative when given specific tasks. That was why Olminsk had picked him to head the operation aboard the cruise ship, and promised to compensate the Vietnamese pirate for any losses in ransom he took when it became necessary to flee the ship in advance of the chemical release.

The chemicals were the key, both to Olminsk's long-term retirement goals, and to something he considered much more important—his revenge. He was only just beginning to come to terms with his new life as, not just a pirate, but a wealthy one, when a chance raid had turned into a miracle.

The freighter they'd seen and attacked, an aging container ship, had made its way from Oman and thence to the Indian Ocean. Olminsk knew now that its nearly incalculable treasure, hidden among the various banal items otherwise filling the ship's cargo, was destined for North Korea. He had gotten that much from the two Saudis assigned to guard the container, the two men whose presence had tipped him to the possibility of something unusual in the first place. They had died hard, but in the end, they had told him what he needed to know.

Grigori had made them talk. The former KGB man was a total sadist. It had been uncomfortable, watching Grigori work. But in the end it had all been worth it.

A single precious container aboard the ship held specially pressurized canisters. The name of the substance inside was unknown to Olminsk and likely unpronounceable to him. But he understood what it could do. If the two Saudis had been sufficiently truthful in their last moments of life, and Olminsk imagined they had been so, he knew as much as he needed to know.

Developed in Saudi Arabia—Olminsk pictured some Saudi scientist, or group of them, rogue or otherwise—the chemical contained in the canisters was a powerful synthetic acid. Contained within its canisters it was safe enough, but once exposed to air it became virulent. A container the size of a barrel of oil could devastate a city block if spilled. A similar container turned to aerosol by an explosion that sprayed it over an area could kill as a kind of nerve agent, Olminsk understood, affecting an entire region of that city. The substance was so destructive that it *had* to be valuable.

Before he could sell it at what he considered its true price, however, Olminsk had had to arrange for a demonstration. That was the reason for the cruise ship hijacking.

He had poured as much of his resources into the operation as he could, in an effort to ensure its success. He had drawn on all of the surplus Russian technology he could locate through his sources back home. He had spent much money. He had gone so far as to use his personal satellite communicator, knowing that once he gave it to Tranh he was unlikely to see it again for any of several reasons. All of this had been done because he needed to let the world know that the means to strike the devil West were available to those with the money and the courage. It was to have been a glorious blow against Western sensibilities, one that would have struck the Americans directly through the loss of a congressman's family. Olminsk had paid dearly for the information, for knowledge of any high-value Americans traveling within his sphere of influence. When word had come of the two women aboard the *Duyfken Ster,* their presence had sealed the fates of those aboard.

Or so Olminsk had thought at the time.

To have his plan derailed, to have his revenge thwarted, vexed him greatly. He sucked at the cigarette, letting it burn down to the filter, then stubbed it out in the overflowing ashtray beside him. Without thinking he sparked another, using the scarred steel lighter that still bore the etching of his name and naval rank. The lighter was a constant reminder of what he had lost, of what the Soviet Union and the new Russia after it had suffered at the hands of the West.

He *would* make them pay. Some force, some power, some act of fate or chance had put into *his* hands the means to strike back. He had been granted the ability to make the Americans and their allies pay. He had been given an opportunity to make the entire industrialized world regret the ill destiny that had befallen Mother Russia and her people.

He would not be stopped.

Tranh had failed. That much was obvious, though the authorities had blacked out coverage of the cruise ship. After the transmission, which Olminsk had monitored through his own black-market receiver, there had been no follow-up. News that the hostages had been freed trickled out shortly thereafter, but there was no footage, no coverage of the mop-up. Local news outlets had already expressed their disgust at their governments' unwillingness to show the results of the pirate raid. Olminsk understood that there had been much death among the crew especially, and thus he understood the squeamishness with which those in power now dealt with the attack. But what had happened to Tranh? How had his entire crew been lost? The usual means of contact had revealed nothing. Tranh, the woman Merpati, the technician Noor and all the others could not be reached, not by radio and not by satellite phone. It was if they had disappeared off the face of the earth.

The reality was, of course, that they had likely sunk to the bottom of the sea. There must have been, Olminsk had to admit, some flaw in his plan, some gap. Somehow a counterterrorist or law-enforcement team of some kind had taken the ship back, freeing the passengers and the remaining crew. Tranh and his people had failed. Olminsk supposed that it had been too much to ask of the cunning little Vietnamese, to run what was essentially a military operation.

There was no point in dwelling on the failure. All he could do was deal with the results. The message had been sent, and if no demonstration was forthcoming, he would look the fool. None of the potential customers who might seek a weapon of such power would take him seriously, and certainly none would pay his price. It was therefore necessary to strike out hard, to make an even greater example.

He had lost the ability to use the aging satellite network, with the loss of his communicator. He would have to compensate for that, too. The only option was a public display, something so great and so terrible that news of its details could not be suppressed. An isolated shipboard incident would not do, though it had its attractions—for Olminsk could easily field the men and equipment needed to seize another ship. No, he needed something on land, something local, something spectacular.

The chemicals were stockpiled in Semarang. He would move a portion of them to a public target, one of the landmarks of the Old City. And there he would demonstrate the power of the chemicals, releasing a new message to the world through public news and data channels. He would confirm that those responsible for the *Duyfken Ster* were behind this new act. In that way he would gain the customers he required to sell off the rest of the chemicals. Then he could retire in luxury in some other tropical location, sipping drinks on a beach while hearing of the latest gas attack on Western citizens. That would be his legacy. Olminsk would not allow himself to relax, to enjoy the wealth he would accumulate, until he knew that the chemicals had made their way into the hands of those who hated the West as much as did he.

Then he would sleep happily at night, for many long nights, a rich man with no past and a leisurely future.

The *Milaya Volya* would make port in Semarang shortly. Olminsk left the bridge to check the small mess, where his most loyal crew prepared themselves for the work to come.

What was most important was that he could count on them to do what had to be done. All were bitter about the great nation they had once served becoming a shadow of its former self. All sought revenge. This united them. This was their common purpose, beyond profit, beyond thoughts of luxury and leisure in their later years.

They would have that revenge. Olminsk would see to it.

Vasily Radchinko was the nominal leader of the group, after Olminsk and in Grigori's absence. A dour man of average height, he had the ugliest, craggiest face Olminsk had ever seen. Radchinko was cruel and quick to anger, but also a very good fighter. As Olminsk looked on, he stripped the Kalashnikov on the table in front of him, doing so by rote, his habits ingrained in the Soviet military. He had been naval Special Forces, which was why Olminsk valued him.

Playing with an AK bayonet, which Olminsk knew had been painstakingly sharpened to a near hair-splitting edge, was Timofei Maevsky. Maevsky was petulant and volatile, but one of the best knife fighters Olminsk had ever seen. These were skills honed out of boredom aboard ship, as there was little call for such skills. Olminsk sometimes wondered if Maevsky had somehow foreseen his future as a brigand and prepared accordingly.

Kirill Chebykin, the large one, sat at the end of the mess table with his head in his hands. He was asleep. Chebykin had the strange ability to sleep almost on command, in any position and at any time. Olminsk had heard of this ability in some veteran soldiers, but he was unsure of its genesis in Chebykin. It did not matter. Chebykin was a heavy-weapons expert and had rigged the detonator charges for the chemicals sent with Tranh for the cruise ship hijacking. Olminsk knew the man was disappointed that they had not exploded. He delighted in such conflagrations, even the thought of them. Once, during their naval days, Olminsk had dug deeply into Chebykin's files.

The man had been a pyromaniac as a child, one who enjoyed starting fires for the sake of watching them. He had grown out of those childish impulses, as far as Olminsk knew. But the Russian captain was still careful not to use his cigarette lighter in Chebykin's presence, if he could help it.

Leonid Jaburov, the calm one, sat reading a book, ignoring the activity around him. Olminsk knew from experience that Jaburov would already have checked his weapons and resigned himself to whatever was to come. He had been a high-ranking officer under Olminsk, once, and was then and now the most humorless man Olminsk had ever met. He did his work, and even the more brutal aspects of piracy, with neither joy nor disdain. He did whatever Olminsk asked of him without comment. The Russian captain wondered how it was that such a man could go through life without experiencing a moment of happiness. There were times when Olminsk expected to find the other man dead by his own hand, but Jaburov continued on, day after day. Olminsk did not have to understand it as long as Jaburov continued to do his work.

The last of his trusted crew, Ilya Favorsky, smiled at Olminsk as he cleaned his pistol. The weapon was a gold-plated .50-caliber Desert Eagle with pearl grips, as ostentatious a handgun as Olminsk had ever seen. Ilya thought himself a gunfighter and carried the massive, ridiculous gun in a hand-tooled leather holster tied to his thigh. When he was not working or enjoying the fruits of their piracy, he was reading American Westerns and perfecting his horrid interpretation of Western slang. Olminsk could forgive these bizarre traits in the man, for he was truly a very good shot, not to mention a fast draw. More than once his ability with a gun had enabled him to kill Olminsk's enemies before those enemies could draw a bead on Olminsk himself. The Russian captain was nothing if not practical.

"We make port in Semarang soon," he told the men.

"Orders?" Radchinko asked.

"I will choose a location for the demonstration," Olminsk promised. "We must strike quickly. It will be a public place in Semarang."

"But, Captain," Jaburov remarked, "If we strike at our own port, will that not work against us in the long run?"

"There is no long run, not if this works," Olminsk said. "We shall be rich men, and we shall retire."

8

Suharto's driver brought Bolan and the Indonesian intelligence operative to a loading and unloading area near the Tawang rail station. Suharto and the Executioner made their way inside, past a newsstand and snack shop, through the glass doors. Bolan's boots were loud on the highly polished, tiled floor.

The platform area was impressive enough, with advertising banners dotting the support posts. Planters bearing local greenery were set every few dozen feet. Ramps up the steps to the platform had been placed almost haphazardly after the fact to provide access for wheelchairs and carts. Here and there on the platform were tables and wheeled carts, devoid of merchandise, whose purpose was unknown to Bolan. He assumed they were used either by local merchants or for some other public purpose.

Near a blue plastic barrel that Bolan assumed was for refuse or recycling, Suharto's informant waited under an advertising banner for an Indonesian clove cigarette. Suharto and Bolan approached and began walking with the man, who fell into step beside them without comment. Around them, those waiting for trains, debarking, or hurrying to meet those trains coming in swirled past. Tawang station, like all other parts of Semarang Bolan had seen, pulsed with life.

"This is Idyan," Suharto said as they walked. Bolan noted with approval that Suharto made no attempt to identify Bolan for the informant in any way. He might not be a veteran gunhand, but the Indonesian was a capable intelligence operative.

They made a casual circuit through the rail station foot traffic, with Suharto nominally leading them. Anyone who had them under direct surveillance would eventually notice the pattern they walked, Bolan supposed, but if they were already under direct surveillance, they would not be fooling anyone for long, anyway.

"Your report, Idyan?" Suharto asked.

"It is not good," Idyan said, his English more heavily accented than Suharto's but still quite good. "The Saudis are very motivated to intercept the chemicals before any other force may do so."

"Yes, we are quite aware," Suharto said wryly.

"You do not understand," Idyan said. Bolan noticed he was sweating heavily. It was hot, but he would have thought the locals accustomed to it.

"What do I not understand?" Suharto said.

"The Saudi security forces have conducted a series of raids on locations known to be connected to Olminsk," Idyan said. "They are working from a list more comprehensive than our own. They have hit several locations about which we knew nothing."

"This is bad news, certainly, but not unexpected," Suharto said. "Their resources are more extensive than our own. Their methods are also more ruthless than those we employ."

"They have Dr. Wahid."

"What?" Suharto started.

"Who is Wahid?" Bolan asked.

"A chemist attached to UNDIP," Suharto said.

"UNDIP?"

"Diponegoro University," Idyan said.

"He has intelligence credentials," Suharto admitted.

"He has advised us before. As you can imagine, a chemist is most useful in analyzing certain substances, such as explosives. We have used him in that capacity. He was working on the problem of the Saudi acid."

"Our people are working on that, as well," Bolan said. "We have to look at hard realities here. Could he have been that much farther along or that much better?"

"Eh...you still do not understand," Suharto said, looking embarrassed. "We uncovered certain data in our investigation of Olminsk's holdings here."

"What information?"

"One of the places we were able to examine, in secret, is a storage facility rented by one of Olminsk's holding companies. It included a very, very small sample, a trace amount, of the acid. We are not certain why it was left there, but we believe Olminsk himself had the chemical analyzed by some outside agency, perhaps to verify its nature independently, or perhaps even in some vain quest to see if he could reproduce it from the sample. This was probably done outside the country and is beyond our means to pursue. We did find shipping materials and manifests to support our theory. But there was enough of the trace chemical left, hermetically sealed in a protective vial, for us to attempt a chemical analysis of our own."

"Why," Bolan said, his jaw clenching, "would something so valuable be left behind?"

"We believe it was an oversight," Suharto said. "Something left by a careless underling, who did not think the remaining material important enough to bother with after leaving it hidden in storage."

"And your possession of an actual chemical sample of the gas?" Bolan asked angrily. "Was that an oversight?"

"Please understand, Mr. Cooper," Suharto said, shaking his head. "Santoso Wahid is an expert in his field and an employee of my government. His position with the university is simply for public consumption. He works from a fully equipped laboratory with all the safety and analytical equipment required to produce a solution. We had thought that if anyone could provide a means of dealing with the Saudi chemical agent, he could."

"And score points?" Bolan asked.

"Something like that," Suharto admitted. "Our government is already sensitive about outside involvement in our affairs, as you can imagine. It was only with reluctance that they agreed to assign me to you. These decisions are made at the highest levels of my organization. It is beyond my control."

"So the Saudis abducted Wahid to stop him from making them look bad? All part of their campaign to undo and cover up what Olminsk is trying to accomplish."

"We believe so, yes," Suharto said.

"How did they take him?" Bolan asked.

"He was kidnapped from the secure facility where he was working," Idyan said. "It is a secret location."

"How did the Saudi security forces know about it, then?" Bolan persisted, asking the obvious question.

"We have a leak in our organization," Suharto answered, shrugging.

"Yes, we do," Idyan said. From under his shirt he drew a .38-caliber revolver, thrust it into Suharto's chest and pulled the trigger. The Indonesian intelligence operative bleated something incomprehensible and went down, the smell of the fired cartridge thick in the air. Idyan turned to fire another a shot at Bolan, but the soldier was already moving. He fired a vicious palm heel into Idyan's chin while grabbing the cylinder of the revolver in a death grip, preventing it from turning.

Nearby travelers and commuters screamed. The gun shot

set off a panic. Idyan, reeling, chose not to fight for control of the weapon. Instead he simply let go and bolted. Bolan tracked the fleeing man through the thickening morass of frightened locals and tourists. He did not dare draw one of his own weapons. Tossing the fouled revolver into the nearby trash barrel, he went after the informant-turned-assassin.

Idyan threw himself off the platform and onto the train tracks below. He began to run. Bolan charged after him, only too aware that armed security officers could descend on them at any moment. If that happened, he would be unable to defend himself. He would not shoot local law enforcement or security forces simply for doing their jobs.

Idyan ran swiftly. The tracks passed through an access yard and maintenance depot, where the informant fled. Bolan followed, hot on the heels of the Indonesian.

He ran right into a trap.

The dark suits and headgear that marked them unmistakably as Saudi security gave the waiting team away as soon as he saw them, but Bolan knew he was not meant to leave alive. It would not matter, therefore, what he saw or heard, for he would never get the chance to speak of these if the Saudi team had its way.

He analyzed the tactical situation in the split second he had to take in the scene. The maintenance depot was a long, open, high-ceilinged shelter with repair bays to either side for railcars and engines. The lighting was dim. The equipment to either side formed perfect cover for the waiting gunners now drawing a bead on Bolan.

Idyan was caught in the middle.

The Saudis opened fire. Automatic weapons strobed in the semidarkness of the depot's shadows. Bolan ran, first going straight for Idyan, then throwing himself to the side. The hapless traitor provided a shield for Bolan, giving him the precious fraction of an instant he needed to get behind a stack of crates. The informant screamed and went down. Bullets pinged from the machine parts in the crates as Bolan crouched, unlimbering his submachine gun and preparing to return fire.

Before he could acquire a target, Bolan heard other voices shouting. He thought it might be Javanese; then he heard the commands repeated in English. The Saudis were being ordered to drop their weapons and surrender.

Gunfire erupted anew. Muzzle flashes lit the flickering hellscape in shades of yellow and bright orange. The noi : was deafening. When the last of the shells hit the gravel floor of the depot Bolan turned to move. As he did so, he was confronted by four men clad in navy blue coveralls and wearing full tactical gear—ballistic load-bearing vests, flared steel helmets, goggles and gloves. The automatic weapons they held trained on the Executioner were U.S.-made M-16s.

The counterterrorist team shouted commands at Bolan. Even before they switched to English he knew what they wanted readily enough. Lacing his fingers behind his head, he situated himself on his knees, making sure they could see he was no threat and would not resist. It would not do to be shot now, with the battle over. He risked a glance around; the Saudis were all down and none of them moved.

The counterterrorist operatives urged him to his feet. One of them moved Bolan's hands behind his back and cuffed him with metal handcuffs. A second frisked him, pausing to eye the soldier with something like amazement as Bolan's various weapons were removed from his person. Eventually one of the men took Bolan's canvas war bag and began piling the weaponry in it, struggling with the heavy bag once it contained both of his pistols, his magazines and the submachine gun.

They were starting to lead him away when Idyan groaned.

"Please," Bolan said calmly. "I must know what this man says, if anything." One of the men looked at him oddly. Only his eyes were visible behind his balaclava, but he seemed to grasp what Bolan wanted. He took the soldier by one arm and led him to the critically wounded Idyan, then stood nearby with his rifle at the ready as Bolan knelt beside the dying informant.

"Idyan," Bolan said. "Why? Why did you do it?"

"They…paid me… The Saudis…"

"To get inside the local investigation? To head it off?"

"Yes…."

"Why did you shoot Suharto and try to kill me?"

"They…paid…to stop the…investigation…" Idyan said. "I didn't…know you would…even be here. They wanted Suhar…Suharto…dead."

"To stop the investigation." Bolan nodded. "Why did you do it?"

"I have no country," Idyan said. "I care…for nothing. I wanted…money. It seemed…so easy."

Idyan died staring into the face of the Executioner, a trickle of blood escaping his lips. Bolan stared into the lifeless eyes and shook his head.

The counterterrorist officers took Bolan by the arm once more, one to either side. They were dragging him toward a waiting van when Suharto came running up, out of breath and clearly in pain.

"Officers!" he was shouting. "Stop, stop!" One of the operatives—Bolan assumed it was the leader of the squad—paused to speak with Suharto in hushed tones as the others continued to lead Bolan to the van. The Indonesian intelligence agent showed some credentials, then continued to talk. The conversation eventually grew heated.

While largely out of earshot, Bolan could hear enough to know that Suharto was angry.

The operatives hustled Bolan into the van. He was placed in a caged prisoner transport area in the back of the vehicle, separated from the rest of the van by a corrugated metal wall. He could feel the doors of the van being opened and closed. When the vehicle started, he was sure he could still hear Suharto's voice, apparently in the passenger seat, arguing with the driver.

Two hours later, the Executioner was seated in an interrogation room in Semarang's police headquarters. From behind a scarred wooden table, he flexed his wrists, working circulation back into them. The officers who had brought him in had only reluctantly taken the cuffs off. He waited patiently, knowing there was nothing else to be done, and counted on Suharto to manage something. Brognola would be none too happy if he had to get involved, but the big Fed would pull the necessary strings if he had to.

When the door opened, it revealed Suharto in the company of another police officer. Suharto, Bolan was pleased to see, was heavily laden with Bolan's war bag.

"Mr. Cooper," Suharto said, placing the bag heavily on the table, "this is Inspector Ramachad. It is through his good graces that you are being released."

Ramachad was a dour, pinch-faced man with small eyes and a bent, worried look. He eyed Bolan with obvious distaste. When he spoke, his accent was heavy. He gestured, the sweep of his arm taking in Bolan's canvas bag.

"These," he said, "are highly illegal for a visitor."

Bolan said nothing.

"Inspector Ramachad has been in touch with the American embassy," Suharto explained, "and in turn with your nation's government. He has spoken with a representative in your Justice Department, as well as several other high-ranking officials."

"It is highly irregular," Ramachad said sourly. "However, we have received special instructions from our government. You have been issued limited credentials." He threw a crumpled sheaf of papers at Bolan, letting them fall to the table. "See that you stay out of the way."

"I—"

Ramachad spun on his heel and walked out before Bolan could manage more than that single word. The soldier stared after him, incredulous.

"He is not happy," Suharto said, rubbing his chest.

"That much is obvious," Bolan affirmed. "Why aren't you dead?"

"Bulletproof vest." Suharto grinned, looking pained nonetheless. "Or perhaps…bullet-*resistant* vest would be the better term. I am told I have a cracked rib, among other indignities. It is very painful, being almost-shot."

"You should try actually being shot sometime," Bolan said.

"I will take your word for it." Suharto shrugged, evidently regretting the gesture as soon as he made it. His face creased in pain.

"Your government has made it clear that we should accept your…assistance," Suharto revealed. "But there is more to it than that. As you will make it in your own report soon enough, and I am not fool enough to try and stop you, I made sure your government knew of the withholding of the chemical sample."

"Why?" Bolan asked.

"Because it is the only way my own government would listen," Suharto said, beginning to shrug and stopping himself. "I will most likely suffer for it. I was not well liked among some of those higher in the administration at any rate. But now they will be very angry. It does not matter. I would sooner stay forever at this station in life than see the acid used on others because I would not speak out."

"You're a good man, Suharto," Bolan said.

"That remains to be seen," Suharto said. "But come, we must get you out of here before they change their minds. They were most interested in your weaponry. I think perhaps they thought to keep this very fancy machine gun. Your government made clear to mine that your materiel was…government property."

Bolan almost laughed at that. He began removing weapons and magazines from the bag, checking the status of each firearm and making sure it dry-fired properly before reloading it, holstering it and strapping it on.

"I was told Idyan was killed," Suharto said sadly.

"He got in the way of his new friends, the Saudis," Bolan said.

"They were all killed, of course," Suharto said. "I am informed that an official protest is being lodged with Saudi Arabia."

"That won't do much," Bolan said.

"No," Suharto replied. "It will not. But the forms must be followed, must they not?"

Bolan nodded. He had seen such scenarios play out before.

"Cooper," Suharto started, then paused. When he continued, he said, "Idyan. Did he…did he say anything? I have worked with him for years. I never would have thought him a traitor, or a killer."

"He told me that he had no country. That he did it for the money."

Suharto looked thoughtful. "I suppose that is as good an answer as one could expect."

"Would he have lied to us?" Bolan asked. "The information he gave us—how likely is it that he told us the truth?"

"I do not think he lied, no," Suharto said. "Dr. Wahid is indeed missing. Idyan was never what I would have considered particularly creative or imaginative. I suspect he simply delivered the report he would have delivered in any case, and then tried to kill us to collect the price he was promised. I wonder how much he thought he was getting."

"Does it matter?"

"I suppose not," Suharto said. "I am still surprised he would have done something like that. I would like to think it was a lot of money. To say he had no country... I always thought better of him than that. I guess you never really know. I suppose I am simply glad that it was nothing personal."

"It often isn't," Bolan said. "That doesn't make him any less dead. Come on—" he stood "—let's get the hell out of here."

"Indeed," Suharto said, still rubbing his chest. "There remains work to be done."

9

Yasud Gafar closed the phone he carried and placed it in the breast pocket of his dark, double-breasted suit. He adjusted the sunglasses shielding his eyes, checked that his *igal* held his red-and-white checkered *ghutra* properly in place on his head, and paused to regard himself in the mirror on the hotel room's door. He opened his coat and slightly adjusted the inside-the-waistband holster bearing his 9 mm CZ-75 pistol. Opposite that, behind his left hip, he carried twin inside-the-waistband pouches for spare magazines, in which he kept fifteen rounds each. Strapped to his leg under his right pants leg was a custom-made *jimbaya*. He knew he was well-armed.

That might not be enough.

Force of arms alone, at least as one man, was no match for the power that could be brought to bear on him by his government. As a team leader for the Saudi elite security force, Gafar was intimately familiar with how tenuous a hold any operative held on this world. Failure meant death and, worse, it meant a dishonorable death, denied paradise.

Not that Gafar was particularly religious. He repeated the words as well as anyone, but in his heart, he believed in little save the reality of what must be done. Many of his men were staunch Muslims, of course, and they believed him to be, as well. It did no harm for them to think so. His task was to manage them, to guide them to success in whatever objective they were granted.

And that was the issue.

His men had failed. Not once, but twice. They had had the interlopers in their sights and they had failed to eliminate them. This was quite unacceptable. For the damage to Saudi Arabia to be contained, this Suharto and the American Cooper with him had to be stopped. The chemicals could not be recovered by the Americans or the local authorities. Saudi Arabia's honor was at stake. Saving face for the government was at stake. And Gafar's own head was at stake. If he failed and somehow survived his mission, he would be beheaded, and his family would be executed immediately if they were *fortunate*.

He tensed at the soft knock on the door. Yusef let himself in. The other man, who wore the local dress of a Javanese in sandals and long *batik* shirt, froze where he stood. Gafar realized he had his hand in his coat, on the butt of his gun. He removed the hand and took a deep breath.

"You are nervous?" Yusef asked in Arabic. He held a small wireless phone in his hand.

"I am on edge, yes," Gafar admitted. "And so should you be."

"To what purpose?" Yusef asked. The veteran security operative and bodyguard sat down in one of the hotel room's chairs, leaning on the small breakfast table and passing the phone across to Gafar. "Take it," he said. "I have received and downloaded the information you requested."

Gafar sat and took the phone, willing himself not to shake with pent-up anxiety. He scrolled through the text files and small photos as he read the words on the phone's tiny screen, engrossed despite himself.

"Give me a synopsis," he ordered his subordinate, never taking his eyes from the small, bright screen.

"We know that the man seen with Suharto answers to the name Matthew Cooper," Yusef said.

"Is he a CIA operative?"

"Possibly," Yusef said.

"What do we know of him?"

"Very little," Yuscf said. "Our counterparts at home tell us that their computer searches and data sifting have met with unusual resistance."

"What do you mean?"

"Our specialists say that attempts to correlate data on this Cooper invariably meet with failure after a few attempts. It is as if, according to the technicians, his identity and activities are being actively guarded by some agency, some entity with access to massive computer-processing power. As soon as data is located, it is eradicated actively. The few references we were able to find come from the American press, whose archives are, for the most part, not subject to government oversight."

"The CIA, then." Gafar nodded. "I have not heard of this technique used before."

"Our people say they have never seen its like," Yusef said. "But they do speculate that perhaps it has been in use for some time. We do not know how advanced the Americans might be in this regard, but it is clear they have an advantage."

"We can only do what we can do," Gafar said grudgingly. "Very well. What of Wahid?"

"He remains at work in the lab you had set up for him," Yusef answered. "Under heavy guard, of course. I do not understand why we do not simply kill him."

"Is that so hard to grasp?" Gafar said angrily. "The man is a genius. His skill with chemicals is vastly underrated by many who should know better. I have seen his research."

"You are not a chemist."

"Neither am I stupid," Gafar spat, "and you forget your place."

"Many apologies, brother."

"No matter," Gafar said, placated. "It is clear he has made more progress than anyone we have employed to date. And he now works for his life, not for money and not for country."

"Why do we need him at all?" Yusef asked. "We cannot have him operating, analyzing the chemical, coming up with something to neutralize it. We cannot have him discussing it at all. We should simply make him disappear, and his research with it. That would end the threat he represents."

"It would," Gafar said, sighing, "but not the threat the chemical represents."

"I do not understand."

"It is classified information," Gafar said. "The weapon was hidden away and all evidence of its existence destroyed, not because it is too powerful—there can be no such thing in war on the infidels—but because *we* could not control it. In sufficient quantities it achieves a chain reaction that we find unpredictable. And while in storage it is relatively stable, in time it may grow more volatile. We have some evidence of this, some early laboratory accidents. Those canisters could detonate under their own power, without external explosions to start the reaction."

"Why not destroy any existing stockpiles, then?"

"In small quantities this can be done," Gafar said. "And it is being done. One assumes the Indonesians have destroyed the canisters found about the *Duyfken Ster* in that manner. But the true amount of stockpiled weapon within the nation of Saudi Arabia, as well as some stored with our allies in Syria is too great."

"Too great?" Yusef looked astonished. "But that would have to be an amount bordering on…it is—"

"Yes," Gafar interrupted. "It is that much. The weapon was produced first in secret by a team of scientists working with more zeal than sense. It was then embraced by certain factions within the government who were not aware of the full risks. It was easily enough created. The long-term danger was not understood. For us to destroy the full quantity of it, in portions deemed safe, would take years, and should have started long ago. It still might, of course, but no one is quite sure how long we have left before the chemicals become too volatile to store."

Yusef stared in open amazement.

"Yes," Gafar said. "It is quite insane. But that is the situation. Do you honestly think a single chemist analyzing a small sample of the weapon would warrant such direct measures, if he could not offer much more? Wahid is perhaps the leading scientist in his field, though this is not well-known. He was taken in order to solve this problem for us."

"Do we…" Yusef said hesitantly. "Do we know how the weapon became loose?"

"Greed," Gafar said. "A significant quantity of it was liberated by a member of government, a member who has since met with…an accident."

"To what purpose?"

"To sell, of course," Gafar said. "The idiot thought to sell the weapon to the North Koreans. Even if it was not unstable, the results would have been disastrous."

"I can well imagine."

"So you see that while we have the opportunity open to us, we must use this Wahid."

"Will we let him go free when we are done?"

"*He* thinks so," Gafar said.

"That is not an answer."

Gafar looked at his subordinate, who happened also to be his younger brother. "Yusef," he said, "the man will know far too much about what has occurred. Do you propose to leave him alive? You were ready to kill him simply for having analyzed a sample."

"True," Yusef admitted.

"Recommendations?"

"We know that Indonesian Intelligence withheld from the Americans their knowledge concerning, and possession of, the recovered sample of the weapon on which Wahid started his work."

"And we owe this to the operative we were able to turn," Gafar said. "A fitting end to a traitor, to die in a pit of his own making. The loss of our men grieves me."

"In their defense, brother," Yusef said, "they were there for backup, not to trap the American. The fool informant panicked and led the American right to them, and of course only after trying and failing to kill Suharto as he had been paid to do. But their loss was not in vain. Had Abbas not remained hidden from view and escaped the disaster, we would not have knowledge of this Cooper's involvement. If not for that, and for the traitor Idyan's information, we would be ignorant of the Americans' ongoing interference."

"So? What is your point?" Gafar asked.

"They are so eager to interfere, this Cooper and the Western lapdog Suharto," Yusef said. "Why not let them?"

"Make your point, Yusef."

"I am surprised you do not see it," Yusef said. "We leak to them the location of the laboratory."

"But we need the laboratory," Gafar said. "We *must* have the solution Wahid is close to providing."

"You have just said yourself, he is close to finding a neutralizing agent, or some solution," Yusef countered. "And there is no time to formulate an alternative location, not if you wish to carry out the operation. Make use of what you have. As you have always taught me, is this not strength? To place a lever against the boulders of your fortifications, and use them to rain down death on the enemy?"

"We set a trap, then," Gafar said. "We lure them to the location, and even as Wahid toils, we eliminate those searching for him."

"Exactly," Yusef said. "We get everything we have been sent to procure. We kill the American and Suharto, thus eliminating those on the trail of the weapon. We find the solution and then kill Wahid. We eliminate all other known evidence of the weapon. The Indonesians and even the West may accuse us, of course. But the men we have lost are already dead. They were dead before ever they came to this land. Saudi Arabia will deny all knowledge of them. They are a dead end. Without the American and Suharto, without the scientist Wahid, without the sample we recovered when we took him, we shall have closed that part of the loop. All that remains is finding Olminsk and his criminals."

"That is no small task in itself," Gafar said. "It worries me, this business with the cruise ship. Already his satellite transmission has caused much distress."

"But without the demonstration he promised," Yusef said, "he will be disbelieved. We actually have the Americans to thank for that, brother, if our suspicions bear out. Who else would mount such an attack on a ship held hostage? For all we know it was this Cooper himself, and from what little I have been able to uncover, I could believe it."

"Fool," Gafar shook his head. "Clearly the Americans or perhaps even the Dutch fielded a counterterrorist team."

"Perhaps," Yusef said. It was obvious he was not convinced.

"We must first eliminate the American, and also this Suharto," Gafar said, allowing his thoughts to gel aloud. "But they are the distraction. Olminsk and his *pirates* remain our primary goal."

"Indeed," Yusef agreed. "So we must ask ourselves what he is likely to do."

"The chemical is probably here in Semarang," Gafar said. "Our investigation points to this. We have no evidence of it being hidden elsewhere. All of Olminsk's resources are concentrated here. His warehouses, his business holdings, his contacts and other aspects of trade. We will reorganize and produce a new strike team to replace the one we lost at Tovarisch Imports. I will need you, brother, to lead that team. I am short of men."

"I will do it gladly, of course," Yusef said.

"Good," Gafar replied. He removed his sunglasses and looked his brother in the eyes. "Good," he said again, "because if we fail, our masters will kill you slowly while I watch, and they will make your death look like a blessing when it comes to mine."

The warehouse in the Terboyo industrial estate was like a hundred other facilities used for a hundred other similar purposes. The Executioner had seen many like it in his personal war. The dilapidated building meant to keep rain and trespassers out, squatted amidst similar structures in functional, ugly, commercial solidity. There was a badly damaged pickup truck parked out front, held together by primer and rust putty. In its short bed were several crates.

Bolan and Suharto, concealed behind a nearby concrete block storage building, watched as two men loaded crates from within the warehouse. While they could not hear the conversation, it was clear the men were not Indonesian locals. Both were Caucasian and larger than the local norm.

"Pirates?" Suharto asked.

"You said this warehouse is held by a company run by Olminsk," Bolan said.

"Yes."

"Then I'm betting pirates," Bolan confirmed.

The smaller and louder of the two men wore a lightweight three-quarter-length overcoat despite the heat. He paused to scratch at himself. Bolan caught sight of the butt of a gun riding low on his thigh. The man shouted something to the other man, something Bolan could hear. Russian. The other man, from within the warehouse, was shouting something back, also in Russian. So these were likely more of Olminsk's personal crew, dispossessed Russian naval officers or simply countrymen who had gravitated to the pirate captain, Bolan surmised.

"What do you think they are doing?" Suharto asked.

"From the weight of those crates," Bolan said quietly, watching the two men struggle to load one of the wooden boxes, "and from the dimensions, I'm willing to bet there are weapons inside."

"Ah, you mean conventional weapons."

"Yes," Bolan said. "Guns. Perhaps some explosives. They're gearing up for something."

"This does not look good," Suharto said. "Do you suppose the failed attempt on the cruise ship now drives them to more desperate measures?"

"Yes," Bolan said. He watched grimly. With no other leads to follow and the trail relatively cold, the Executioner had decided to return to Suharto's list. His theory at the time had been that Olminsk's resources remained what they were, regardless of others' knowledge of them. If the pirate leader intended to use what was available to him locally, harassing and surveilling those resources remained the best option for acquiring him or his men. Bolan had not expected this strategy to pay off so quickly, but then, combat was fluid and unpredictable in that way. He had long ago learned to be equally psychologically fluid, mentally flexible, in order to adapt to the constantly changing combat landscape.

He and Suharto were presented with two enemies with potentially valuable information.

The men were finishing their loading even as the pair watched. There was no time to call for backup. Bolan didn't have anyone to call, at any rate. Local law enforcement was none too happy to have him on site, and while Brognola was no doubt leaning heavily on them, they would offer their cooperation only reluctantly. He could not trust them to do as he needed, or to follow his instructions.

Suharto's intelligence agency likewise was understaffed and not supported by the government regime in place. Had they manpower to spare Bolan would not know who among them he could trust.

With the numbers falling, it was up to Bolan and Suharto alone to intercept the two Russians. Bolan checked his weaponry, in place under his tunic, and motioned to Suharto. Suharto produced his sawed-off shotgun once more, looking resolute but terrified, and nodded. Bolan made walking motions with his fingers, indicating Suharto should take the rear. He pointed to his own chest and then motioned straight ahead. He would go in directly, drawing the Russians' attention and likely their fire. They had already discussed the importance of taking at least one of the men alive, if they could. That meant Suharto was to use the shot loads in his cut-down double-barrel to aim for the legs, hopefully disabling one or both before they could do serious damage.

It was a risky plan, but Bolan had seen more than his share of risky plans during his war.

As Suharto began to work his way around, unseen, Bolan stepped out to charge straight ahead. That was when he heard an engine. Chance, always potentially lethal, had reared its ugly head. A small, seen-better-days four-wheel drive vehicle was trundling into the parking area near the warehouse, making its way through the maze of shipping containers and other vehicles left to bake in the sun outside the building. It stopped directly in the Executioner's line of fire, blocking the pickup from his view.

Bolan flattened himself against the wall, hoping they had not seen him—and hoping Suharto would have the sense to stay out of sight when he did not hear the planned diversion.

One of the four men in the truck, who from Bolan's quick glance appeared to be Indonesians, began to shout something, sounding agitated.

They had seen him.

Bolan unlimbered his submachine gun and broke cover, bringing the deadly, compact weapon to bear on the small truck. The men inside were already scrambling out and ducking for cover, weapons in their hands.

Bolan's gun sprayed jacketed slugs into the lower panels of the truck, taking out the tires and wreaking havoc in the engine compartment. There was no way to judge the extent of the damage, but his immediate purpose was simply to neutralize the vehicle and take it out of play.

One of the Indonesians, slower than his counterparts, had taken cover behind the truck instead of among the shipping containers or inside the warehouse. Bolan paused just long enough to sight beneath the vehicle, flicking on the laser unit. As he did so, the man behind the four-wheel drive began to fire his own pistol, an old Makarov. The surplus Communist-bloc weapon was no less deadly than Bolan's modern hardware.

The green dot of the laser danced over the gunner's knee as the man crouched behind the dubious safety of the truck. Bolan triggered the weapon in two-round burst mode. The gunner began screaming, writhing out from behind the truck as the sudden trauma made him forget his precarious position. Bolan put a single round through his head.

The Russians had regrouped. The smaller one in the light overcoat had joined the Indonesians among the shipping containers out front. They began to concentrate their fire on Bolan's position, driving him around the corner of the building. A cloud of concrete dust filled the air as their small arms fire—from pistols and an ancient wood-stocked

Uzi wielded by one of the Indonesians—riddled the face of the wall Bolan was using for cover. The corner began to chip away, driving Bolan back.

He could hear a vehicle starting and assumed it was the pickup. There was nothing he could do while pinned down. The gunners kept hosing the corner of the building and, when Bolan could finally see the truck from his vantage point, it was already passing behind other cover as it made its way out of the artificial maze surrounding Olminsk's warehouse.

Bolan's jaw tightened. He remained behind cover as the gunners hammered away, waiting them out. The lull came, almost before he expected it. The shooters ran dry. They were either too inexperienced or too arrogant to stagger their reloads. Bolan charged out from cover, weapon spraying, driving the shooters behind their own barriers.

The Executioner followed his rounds in, chasing after the flying bullets until he was in the midst of the shooters. He drew the Beretta 93-R left-handed and, with the submachine gun in his right fist, he opened fire to both sides as he punched through. It was sloppy and wildly dangerous, but his opponents were in no way prepared for the blitz. He managed to tag two of the Indonesians and drive the third back into the warehouse. The man ran on the heels of one of the Russians, the one in the coat.

Bolan bulled his way through, using his shoulder to shove the heavy door aside. The interior of the warehouse was much darker than the bright tropical day outside. He squinted and dodged instinctively, even as bullets rang out from somewhere within. They did not come close. Bolan found himself among canyons of rusting metal shipping containers stacked dozens of feet high. Olminsk could have been hiding anything inside, perhaps even the Theta-Seven.

Crouching to make his silhouette as small as possible,

Bolan put his back to a crate and waited for his eyes to adjust. He allowed himself to go completely still, blending with the shadows, waiting to hear, taste and smell what his hunter's senses could tell him.

He did not wait long.

The lone Indonesian, while armed and certainly dangerous, was no match for a trained and experienced soldier. The man blundered about in the dim light, trying to be quiet, but he made so much racket scuffing his shoes and bumping into things that Bolan was aware of him every moment. What he *couldn't* hear was any sign of the other man, the Russian in the coat. That worried him. It was possible the Russian was waiting for Bolan to take the Indonesian, which meant the other man was being used as bait. That was as cold as it was potentially effective. Bolan decided to bide his time. There wasn't much of it, but he couldn't afford to stop a bullet, either.

And where was Suharto?

Bolan waited. Five minutes passed, then ten. Finally, the Russian broke, his need to take Bolan overwhelming his sense of caution.

"You there!" the Russian called in accented English. "I know you are here!"

There was a scraping sound nearby, to Bolan's left. That would be the Indonesian, starting at the sound of the Russian's voice. The man was smaller and moved much more tentatively than the Russian in the coat. Bolan had been able to judge that much just from seeing them both move.

"Come out, big man!" the Russian called, his tone mocking. "Or do you fear?"

Bolan remained silent. There were some echoes that made it more difficult to tell, but he was fairly certain he had placed the man in the coat, to his right and forward.

The remaining Indonesian, meanwhile, was moving around somewhere behind and still to the left. The threat he represented was relatively low. Bolan took no action, however. He did not dare give away his position. The Russian was an unknown threat.

Why, he wondered, had the local police not shown up yet? The gunfire would have alerted anyone in the area. One or two shots might be overlooked in an industrial area like this one, but a protracted gunfight? There was no way someone would not have called the authorities by now.

He was, nevertheless, grateful not to have to deal with outside interference.

"Where are you?" the Russian called. He was at the far end of the warehouse, from what Bolan could tell. He spotted the Indonesian running out the door. "Come out, Hoss," he said. "Of course you are there. Let us settle this like men." Bolan could hear the voice coming closer.

"Cooper," Suharto called out, sounding embarrassed.

"Oh, did I not mention?" The Russian laughed. "I have a member of your posse here! Come out or I put a bullet through the back of his head."

Bolan emerged from the shadows. He held the laser of the submachine gun on target, the green dot floating over Suharto's shoulder as he tried and failed to track the Russian behind him.

"Oh, no," the man said, "I do not think so. You are not going to try trick shooting on me, *Pardner!*" The Russian laughed again as he crouched behind Suharto. He held a very large, very shiny Desert Eagle—.50 caliber, Bolan noted—to the back of Suharto's skull. He was careful to stay behind the man and offered nothing the Executioner could shoot without endangering the intelligence operative.

"Let him go," Bolan said. "You shoot him, I shoot you."

"I am sure you would!" the Russian said. "Or at least you would try. But I have something else in mind."

"I'm listening."

"I have always wanted to match myself against one such as you," the Russian admitted. "What did he call you? Cooper?"

"That's right," Bolan said.

"I am Ilya."

"Fine, we're well-acquainted now," Bolan said. "Let him go."

"Perhaps," Ilya said. "Do you know, I have never before met a real cowboy?"

"I'm not a cowboy," Bolan said.

"But of course you are," Ilya said. "You are a gun-slinger. The epitome of those who rode the range and tamed the West."

"If you say so."

"You are anxious to die," Ilya said. "But that is all right. I tell you what. Holster your gun. You cannot shoot me, anyway. When you do, I will holster mine. And I will allow this…this *person*—" the Russian sounded disgusted "—to step out of the way. Then we can face each other as men of boldness were meant to do."

"He does not think much of me," Suharto said. "I got caught."

"You are nothing," Ilya said behind him. "This man before you is the type of gunfighter others fear."

"You would be wise to fear him," Suharto said.

"Be silent!" Ilya ordered. "You know nothing."

"I have watched him kill," Suharto said.

"I said be silent!" Ilya ordered again. He made the smallest movement, as if thinking of drawing back his hand and pistol-whipping the Indonesian intelligence operative. He was good, Bolan had to admit. He had stopped himself, reined in his anger and his urge to lash out, knowing that it might give Bolan the opening he needed.

"The police are coming," Bolan said. "You don't have much time."

"Then neither does he." Ilya shoved his gun slightly, causing Suharto to duck his head. The Russian compensated, crouching even more, keeping Suharto between him and Bolan's deadly guns.

"You don't have to do this," Bolan said.

"But I want to. Holster your gun. If you do so, I will let him go."

"Do not let him kill you," Suharto interrupted.

"Quiet!" Ilya shoved his Desert Eagle forward, hard, into the back of Suharto's skull.

Bolan made a decision. "All right," he said. He pulled his tunic aside, letting the submachine gun fall to the end of its harness. He used his left hand to push the tunic up and over, holding it there with his left arm, to clear the holster for his own .44 Magnum Desert Eagle. His right hand hovered over the butt of the gun.

"You see?" Ilya said, shoving Suharto away and thrusting his own, gaudy weapon into the leather holster on his thigh. "I am a man of my word."

"A rarity," Bolan said.

"Tell me, American," Ilya said, his look almost hungry. "You are obviously a gunfighter, like me. Tell me about the men you have killed. Before it all ends, before I kill you, I wish to know you."

"I haven't been keeping score."

"Of course you have!" Ilya argued. "How could you not? Every life snuffed out, every man shot down, is a man you know is *inferior* to you! He is a man you have bested, a man you have beaten, a man from whom you have taken everything. How could you *not* remember? How could you *not* count?"

"You think a man who kills another is automatically better?" Bolan said.

"Of course," Ilya said. "What else?"

"It doesn't take a good man to pull a trigger," Bolan said. "It doesn't even take a skilled man. The filthiest, most ignorant conscript in the world can fire a Kalashnikov. The stupidest punk on the planet can point a gun and pull the trigger. A lot of good men and women, a lot of *better* human beings, have died at the hands of those who were their inferiors. To murder someone doesn't require much. You just have to have the will to take what you haven't earned."

"When I take your life," Ilya said, "I will have earned it. I have practiced long."

"How many people have you shot?" Bolan asked.

"Enough," Ilya said. "I have painted a mark in the grip of my gun for each one. To date there have been nine. You will be the tenth. It is a position of distinction."

"Nine lives," Bolan said. "Nine people who died because you had something to prove to yourself."

"I have nothing to prove!" Ilya said, becoming angry. "It is you who must prove. You, who must prove that you are better if you are to walk away. We will now have our contest. We will see who wins."

"This isn't the Old West," Bolan said. "And killing is not a game."

"Enough!" Ilya said. "Now we will draw and see who is faster. There is a code among those of the gun—"

"No," Bolan said, "there isn't." Bolan turned suddenly, putting his back to the Russian. The Beretta 93-R chugged out a single round, blowing a ragged hole in the fabric of Bolan's bunched-up tunic and punching the Russian would-be cowboy in the chest. Ilya fell with a squall of pain and surprise. The glittering Desert Eagle skittered across the concrete floor.

Bolan extracted his Beretta from under his tunic. He ejected the 20-round magazine, racked the slide twice to clear the fouled action, then reinserted the mag and jacked a round home. Ilya had been too focused on Bolan's holstered Desert Eagle, too convinced that he was about to get the gunfight he had probably imagined before, to notice Bolan palming the weapon left-handed and moving it across his chest as he shifted his clothing.

"You…" Ilya managed feebly as Bolan came to stand over him. "You *cheated.*"

"This is life and death. It's not a game. I fight to win," Bolan said.

Bolan watched Ilya's eyes go blank.

"This is starting to become a familiar scene," Suharto said quietly. He had retrieved his shotgun from wherever he had dropped it and was breaking it open to insert new shells. Bolan assumed the Russian had made Suharto empty it. "He apprehended me from behind." Suharto shrugged. "When I heard the gunfire start, I decided I had better wait for you to finish what you were doing. I was advancing to help when he caught me."

"It happens," Bolan admitted. "So where *are* the police?"

"That is my fault," Suharto said. "I phoned in and used what little influence I have. I made sure we would not be bothered. I thought you would need time to work, time to extract information. I was told they would look the other way…this once."

"That must have been quite a favor you called in," Bolan said.

"I am not without my contacts in the police department," Suharto said. "And I am not a man without influence, despite the regard in which my agency is held by my government and those who influence it. But I fear I have used up what small leverage I could, and to no avail."

"We'll find them," Bolan said. He walked with Suharto out of the warehouse, his eyes scanning left and right for any threats they might have missed.

"I do not doubt it," Suharto said. "But finding them in time…that is the issue, is it not?"

"It is," Bolan said. "These—" the Executioner nodded to the dead Indonesians near the front door "—must be local talent. Maybe pirates, maybe just muscle brought in by Olminsk. Probably here to take custody of some of the weapons, or to help with whatever operation Olminsk is planning."

"These crates," Suharto said. "They did not get it all." He knelt and opened the nearest wooden crate, exposing a row of Kalashnikov rifles gleaming under the oil used for storage.

"We can check," Bolan said, "but I'm guessing the chemical weapons aren't here. Those would be top priority for whatever Olminsk is planning, but he had these men moving arms instead. We need to find out where he's keeping the Theta-Seven, before he uses it."

"The fellow I mentioned, the contact at the Tinjomoyo Zoo," Suharto said. "He might know of a location we have not yet found. I know of no other place to search, unless he can provide one."

"Then let's move," Bolan said.

11

Suharto took the lead as they found their way through the zoo, which was busy with locals and tourists enjoying the various animals on display. Bolan watched the families with children, knowing that it was exactly this—human life being lived by good men and women—that he fought so hard to protect.

"It is this way," Suharto said. He led them past a fence marked with various signs, which Bolan assumed meant "staff only." Once beyond the fence they faced a low cinder-block building. Suharto opened the metal door. From the look of the equipment in the rooms they passed, there was a veterinary clinic taking up one end of the structure. At the end of the corridor they came to a small office.

Suharto knocked on the door. "It is me," he said simply. He had called ahead and was expected.

"Yes, Mr. Suharto, come in," Santoso Atunarang said in lightly accented English, opening the glass-paneled office door. "You said you were looking for—"

Bolan stood in the doorway. Atunarang stopped abruptly, looking from the big American to Suharto and back again. The much smaller man was short, bald and dressed in a dirty white coat that bore his zoo credentials. His eyes darted nervously from one man to the other behind round-framed spectacles.

"I will tell you what we are really looking for," Suharto said. "And it is not exotic animals sold illegally from within your zoo's roster."

"Who sent you?" Atunarang demanded.

"You do not need to know," Suharto said. "But the real problem is not me, it is *him*." He nodded to Bolan.

The Executioner knew they were pressed for time. He opted for the direct approach. The Beretta 93-R appeared in his hand, the sound-suppressor long, black and lethal-looking as it pointed at Atunarang's forehead. The little man went cross-eyed trying to look at it. He started to shake.

"What…what is this?" he managed to ask. "What do you want from me? I have no money. If this is a robbery—"

"Olminsk," Bolan said. "The Russian who sold you stolen specimens for your zoo."

"What?" Atunarang seemed genuinely surprised.

"You do remember the man?" Bolan prodded with the gun. Atunarang flinched.

"Yes! Yes of course I remember! It is just…it is not such a terrible crime, is it? I have simply given a good home to those creatures that would otherwise be abused, or left to die, or even eaten!"

"How did you come to have contact with Olminsk?" Suharto asked.

"He found me," Atunarang said, almost sobbing. "He said he had merchandise we might want. He said there would be more. The costs were low, and he paid me to keep it quiet. No one was harmed!"

"We're not interested in you," Bolan said from behind the pistol. "We are trying to find Olminsk. We need to find a warehouse that he uses."

"The one where I pick up the animals?"

"Yes," Bolan said.

"Of course!" Of course I will tell you!" Atunarang rattled off an address. Bolan looked to Suharto, who took out his phone and immediately called it in.

Bolan removed the Beretta's muzzle from Atunarang's forehead. "If you've lied to us," he said, "or if you call anyone to warn them, I will be back."

"I have told you all I know!" Atunarang said. "I promise, I will say nothing!"

Bolan nodded curtly. He and Suharto left.

They took the disguised taxi driven by Suharto's man, this time to the address Atunarang had provided. Suharto received a call from his agency as they rode. He spoke quietly into the phone for a few minutes, listened and then turned to Bolan as he put the device away.

"The warehouse is in the Bugangan industrial estate," he said. "It is not owned by Olminsk, or by any of the companies associated with him. Apparently it is one of the first facilities he secured, according to the rent history provided by the owner. The rent is paid in cash, one month ahead of time, and has been for some years now. There is a very good chance this is the sort of place he would warehouse the Theta-Seven."

Bolan nodded. "We'll need whatever backup you can muster."

"I have alerted the appropriate authorities. They will meet us there."

The warehouse was not as large as the one they had visited previously, and there were no signs of activity immediately There was, however, a new-looking minivan parked in the loading area. Bolan withdrew the Beretta 93-R from under his tunic and press-checked it, verifying that a round was chambered. He motioned to Suharto. The Indonesian pulled his sawed-off shotgun from inside his waistband, broke it and snapped it shut again. He nodded grimly.

The man was learning fast.

They split up, Bolan taking the back of the warehouse, Suharto the front. They had discussed the best play on the way over and determined that, until backup arrived, they had to contain the site as best they could, in the hope of stopping the pirates or their hired guns from moving the chemicals—*if* the chemicals had ever been there, and if they had not yet been moved. Much was riding on this run, but there were no other cards left to play in what had been a bad hand from start to finish.

Bolan crept around to the rear of the warehouse and found an access door. It was unlocked. The rusted metal door squealed badly on neglected hinges.

Inside it was very dark. Shafts of light from small louvered windows left most of the storage space in shadow. Bolan unclipped his tactical flashlight and brought it together with his Beretta in a modified Weaver shooting position, the light below the gun, his wrists crossed. He swept up one aisle and down the next, the stacks of dusty crates and metal shipping containers forming neat rows.

He stopped when he saw the section of floor that had, obviously, been recently cleared.

There were scuff marks and shoe prints in the light coating of dust, but the unmistakable circular outlines of dozens of round objects dotted the floor. The outlines were the right size.

The canisters had been there.

"Cooper!" Suharto called. "I think I heard—"

"He did," a voice said in Russian.

Bolan whirled. He was staring straight into the barrel of a pump-action shotgun. The man behind it had dark, bushy eyebrows set over a large, round face. His eyes were deep and almost passive, his face slack. The shotgun held in his hands might have been a paperweight, for all he seemed to care about it. He was completely calm.

Bolan thought, for a moment, that he might be able to bring the Beretta on target and trigger a shot before the other man could pull his trigger.

"Do not try," the Russian said, switching to heavily accented English. "Make the other one come out."

"I won't do that," Bolan said. "Suharto!" he called. "Get lost!"

The Russian sighed. "That was a bad move," he said. The shotgun steadied in the man's hand as his finger tightened on the trigger.

The blare of the bullhorn jolted them. Voices in Indonesian and Javanese began echoing outside the warehouse. The Russian sighed again, strangely subdued. The conflict was over, as far as Bolan could see. Suharto would be outside informing the police of the standoff taking place inside.

"You won't leave alive," Bolan informed him.

"I was not meant to," the Russian said.

"You were waiting for us?" Bolan asked.

"Yes." The Russian inclined his head and indicated a nearby crate. He sat, his shotgun still trained on Bolan. "My name is Leonid Jaburov. You are American?"

Bolan saw no reason to lie. He nodded.

"You are the one who killed Ilya."

"I am."

"We thought it was the Saudis," Jaburov said. "You are aware of my captain, of course?"

"Olminsk."

"Yes," Jaburov said. "He is an intelligent man. Ruthless in his way. In most respects, he has a good head for business. But I have known since all of this started, that it would be our deaths. I do not mind. I welcome it."

"Is that what you were doing here?"

"Not really." Jaburov shrugged, the shotgun moving in his hands. "And yet, yes. When my captain discovered the Saudi weapon and tortured the men shepherding it, he saw its potential. I looked into his eyes. I know for him it was more than just money. The weapon has great value, yes, but for the captain this has always been more about revenge."

"Revenge?"

"On you, of course," Jaburov said. "The West. America. Its allies. The forces that destroyed the Soviet Union and all that it once represented, all that it once could have offered."

"The Cold War was a long time ago. That's a long time to hold a grudge," Bolan said.

"Is it?" Jaburov asked. "How long have you carried a gun in service to America? You are not one of the children one finds newly enlisted. You are a veteran."

"That's true," Bolan admitted.

Outside, the blare of the bullhorns continued. The Executioner wanted to discover what the Russian knew before the local police raided the building. He hoped Suharto was doing what he could to hold them back. For whatever reason, the Russian wanted to talk. Bolan intended to let him, for as long as he could. If he could get the location of Olminsk and the weapons, or any information of value, this run would not be wasted time.

"I could see our doom in this," Jaburov said. "When those we employ here in port reported attacks by the Saudi security agents, or worse, simply disappeared one by one, we knew that eventually they would find us. The captain has done a reasonably good job of hiding his tracks over the years, as he built his pirate empire, but we all knew it would not last forever. As long as those here in central Java could be bribed to look the other way, as long as our attacks took place in the seas that are so sparsely patrolled, we could sustain this life, such as it is. But when the captain decided to become a terrorist, to trade in the weapons of terrorists…it was only a matter of time before the end came."

"He can be stopped," Bolan said. "Tell me what you know."

"Do not mistake my desire to unburden my soul with a desire to betray my captain," Jaburov said blankly. "We all have our motivations. We all retreat into some means of escape from this miserable world. Vasily plays the good soldier, loyal to the end, willing to fight and die for the captain no matter what. Timofei plays with his knives, fancying himself the lone and invincible warrior. Kirill…Kirill does whatever it is he does. For Ilya, it was his ridiculous cowboy fantasies, his desire to live and die by the gun. A desire you granted him, I suspect."

"It didn't go quite like he thought it would," Bolan said.

"I never thought it would end as he pictured it," Jaburov replied. "But you see, we all have our escapes. For me it is this. The truth. A deathbed confession, if you will, followed by the release that I have long wished would come."

"Tell me what you know," Bolan proposed again. "You mentioned the truth. That's no betrayal."

Jaburov laughed, suddenly. It was an odd sound, coming from so solemn a man. "You have talent, American," Jaburov said. "Whatever you are. Are you the police? A secret agent of some kind, perhaps?"

Bolan said nothing.

"It does not matter." Jaburov sighed. "When the Saudis began raiding our facilities here, we received enough reports from those who survived, or escaped, to know what was happening, and who was likely responsible. The captain had an elaborate plan for first using the chemicals, then selling them."

"The attack on the cruise ship," Bolan said.

"Yes. When that failed, he was determined to make his demonstration here, in Semarang, while there was time. But the Saudis were desperate to stop us, desperate to contain the weapon. They began attacking, finding those places we used, uncovering those people and resources that could be linked to the captain's holdings. Even now, the captain hopes to make his demonstration. But he also hoped to put an end to the Saudis' attacks by stopping them once and for all."

"Here?"

"Here," Jaburov said. "We put out the word to those we thought the Saudis might find. Contacts, fences, brokers. We told them to send the Saudi team here. The chemicals *were* here. If they checked they would find supporting evidence that would make the ruse believable. Here they were to die."

"So Atunarang was told to lie and give us this address."

"That worm? Yes, he was one of them."

"How did you intend to stop an entire security team?"

"With this," Jaburov said. He produced an electronic detonator, similar to the ones Bolan had seen on the canisters aboard the cruise ship. "The building is wired with explosives, all that we had left after making preparations for the demonstration here in Semarang."

Bolan was very still as he watched the device in Jaburov's hand. "There doesn't seem much point," he said, "in blowing up the building to kill one man."

"There does not," Jaburov agreed. "But I must be loyal to my captain. I cannot simply surrender."

"It doesn't have to go down like that," Bolan said.

"I am afraid that it does." Jaburov placed the detonator carefully on the crate. "But I think we both know how it will end. And I am glad of it." He set the shotgun down, then, and without hesitation threw himself at Bolan.

The Russian hit the Executioner with sudden, savage fury, propelling close to two hundred pounds into the soldier's chest. Bolan went down, the Russian on top of him, Jaburov's big fists hammering away like stone mallets.

Bolan knew he was dead on the ground if he stayed there. He bucked, throwing the Russian off balance, doing his best to escape the deadly hold the Russian had on him. Bolan lashed out with his knees and managed to get Jaburov turned over onto his side. The Russian roared and threw himself at Bolan once more, but this time the soldier was ready. He slammed Jaburov with his elbows, driving the Russian back and down.

"Good!" Jaburov said through bloodied teeth. He almost seemed to brighten as they fought, grappling, punching and smashing against the crates. Bolan finally managed a hip throw, tossing the Russian up and over, putting space between the two of them.

When Jaburov struggled to his feet, the Executioner was waiting, his Desert Eagle pointed at the Russian's head.

Jaburov smiled, blood flowing from his nose and from his lip. He was breathing heavily. "Just as I thought."

"You can come quietly," Bolan said, nodding to the wall of the warehouse as a fresh volley of bullhorn orders reached their ears. "The police are waiting."

"And spend my days in a prison here?" Jaburov said. "I do not think so. That is not how I picture my retirement years."

"No choice," Bolan said. "It's over."

"Yes," Jaburov said, reaching behind his back. "It is."

Bolan shot first.

A Makarov pistol clattered to the floor, released from Jaburov's nerveless fingers.

The dead man looked almost happy. Bolan walked away, hoping the Russian had found whatever release it was he'd said he wanted.

12

They had a much easier time extracting themselves from the grasp of the local police than Bolan expected. It was because the Indonesian intelligence agent had just received word from a street informant that Wahid had been located. The Saudis were holding him in an office building in the New City, nestled among the many commercial concerns that seemed to spring up daily in Semarang.

As Suharto's driver rushed them to yet another location where there would undoubtedly be yet another battle, Bolan and Suharto discussed the delicate situation. From what Jaburov had said, Olminsk intended a demonstration with the Theta-Seven in Semarang. They might have only hours, or even less, before that occurred.

To find a way to neutralize the weapon was more critical than ever. But would there be time, even if they recovered Wahid?

"Above all," Bolan said, "we need Wahid alive. Even if he knows anything that can help us it still might be too late. But until we know where Olminsk and his people are, until we can hit them, he's our only option."

"I understand," Suharto said. "Cooper, I must again apologize for the actions of my government. Had we not withheld—"

"It's done," Bolan said. "All we can do now is deal with it."

Suharto nodded.

"This will have to be a soft probe," Bolan said. "We can't afford to bring in the troops on this."

"After the explosives they found ready to blow in the warehouse, I doubt they would be eager to help," Suharto said. The locals were still in the process of defusing the detonators, wired to conventional explosives, that the Russian Jaburov had never had the chance or inclination to use.

"It's just us," Bolan said, "and it's going to get ugly. If you want to pull out, I suggest you do so now."

"I have stayed with it this long," Suharto said. "I have seen much that disturbs me. But I understand why. And we fight now not just for your cause, but for Semarang, my home. I will fight with you."

"Let's do it, then," Bolan said.

The driver delivered them to a nondescript address deep in the New City's thriving commercial sector. Bolan looked around, trying to determine if there was anyone or anything unusual at hand. All he saw was traffic, both vehicle and foot, as the citizens, tourists and businesspeople of Semarang hurried off in the pursuit of commerce.

Bolan waved Suharto on behind him as they entered the building. They had been told that the structure, a multilevel high-rise, housed offices on all its floors. The floor they wanted was the fifth one. Suharto headed straight for the elevators.

"No," Bolan said. "Let's take the stairs."

The soldier was reaching for the door to the stairwell when the door slammed open. Three men in black suits and head wraps stood there, pistols in their hands.

"Back!" Bolan shouted. He kicked the door shut just as gunfire rang out on the other side, the bullets failing to penetrate the heavy metal fire door. Bolan whirled to make the exit, but it was too late. More Saudi security operatives entered through the front door.

"Elevator!" Suharto said, as the doors opened. The two men dashed for the only escape. Bolan managed to drive the enemy back, spraying the foyer of the office building with .45-caliber bullets. He deliberately aimed his shots into the floor to not send bullets out the front of the office and into the crowds of civilians walking past.

The elevator doors came together with aching slowness as Suharto jabbed repeatedly at the "door close" button. Bolan reached past him and hit Floor 5. The Indonesian looked up at him curiously.

"What if it is a trap?" he asked.

"Might as well push right through it," Bolan said.

When the elevator moved, however, it moved down, not up. Whether the Saudis had done something to override it, or if this had been part of the plan all along, Bolan could not say. The elevator traveled to the basement level. Bolan pushed Suharto's shoulder, moving him to the opposite side of the elevator.

"Get ready," the Executioner said. "We're going to come out firing."

When the doors opened, Bolan and Suharto both charged, Bolan on the left, Suharto on the right. The Indonesian had produced his little Beretta Jetfire and was emptying the magazine as the two of them burst from the elevator. Meanwhile, Bolan emptied the thirty-round magazine in his submachine gun. The two men found themselves running down a narrow hallway, with concrete block walls at either side.

They stopped when their weapons ran empty.

There was no one there.

"Impressive," a voice said, the accent subtle but noticeable. It came from speakers set within the walls.

Bolan and Suharto had time to raise their weapons. Metal fire doors, pocked with bullet marks, opened up on both sides of the narrow hallway. The men on the other side held submachine guns and assault rifles. They were dressed as the other Saudis had been. One man walked out from behind the others.

"You may, of course, choose to sell your lives dearly," he said. It was the man who had spoken over the loudspeakers. "But if you do, I will kill Wahid. Lay down your weapons. No matter what, you cannot survive."

Bolan looked to Suharto, then at the odds.

Grimly, he let his weapon fall to the end of its sling. Both men raised their hands.

"A wise decision," the man said. "I am Yusef. I represent the House of Saud. You are now my prisoners. Come with me and you will not be harmed."

Bolan did not for a second believe that, but in the hallway there was no way to fight out successfully. He could take many of the enemy, yes, but against these odds, both he and Suharto would be cut down. Yusef knew it, too, however, for he was eager to leave the enclosed space. That suited Bolan just fine. He would simply bide his time until the appropriate opportunity presented itself.

Suharto and Bolan were ushered up several flights of stairs. When they emerged into an office—on the fifth floor, Bolan noted after counting unlabeled stairwells—they found themselves in an anteroom facing glass interior windows. Beyond those reinforced windows was a gleaming white laboratory. The space looked like nothing so much as a converted medical lab, in fact. Armed Saudis stood in the anteroom and in the lab. A man was bent over chemical test equipment in the laboratory.

"Cooper," Suharto whispered. "It is Wahid."

"Yes," Yusef said, overhearing. "It is indeed Wahid.

And he will continue to work for us." Sunlight from the bright tropical day outside streamed in through exterior windows, flooding the anteroom in natural light. Yusef flinched, his eyes apparently still accustomed to the dim lighting of the basement level. He took a pair of sunglasses from inside his double-breasted suit jacket and slipped them on. Bolan recognized this, and the suits the Saudis wore, for the affectations that they were. He watched and waited.

"Tell us what it is you want," Suharto ventured.

Yusef laughed. "Is it not obvious? This trap was set specifically for you. You two have given us no small amount of trouble. I am still trying to figure out how you managed to take down so many of my men. Tigers of Allah, trained elite security agents of Saudi Arabia. Tell me…" He turned to look directly at Bolan. "I can see what *he* is," he said, indicating Suharto with a jut of his chin. "He is unremarkable. But you. Who and what are you, Cooper? Tell me and perhaps I will spare your life."

"You wouldn't, even if I did," Bolan said.

"Yes," Yusef said, "that is likely true." He regarded Bolan for a moment, facing the soldier. "Now I will have you searched. I know you have many weapons. Do not attempt to resist as we remove them. Do not try to withhold anything. After the search will come an interrogation. Please cooperate." He nodded to one of the security men standing behind Bolan.

Whether by prearranged agreement or through some code word in what he'd said, Yusef had given the kill order. Bolan saw that much in the reflection in Yusef's sunglasses. The man behind Bolan, the one who was supposedly to search him, drew a Beretta 92-F from inside his coat and aimed it at the back of Bolan's head, the barrel mere inches from Bolan's skull.

The Executioner exploded into action. As the gun came up, he was already turning, whipping his body around and bringing his arm up. As he swiveled, he caught the Saudi's gun arm with his own extended arm, pulling over and down, placing a powerful and painful lock on the Saudi's arm. As Bolan swiveled his body, the Saudi had no choice but to turn with him. Bolan applied more pressure and twisted, stripping the Beretta out of the man's hand, the big grip filling his own fist.

"Look out!" Yusef shouted.

Bolan emptied the weapon. He fired instinctively, flipping the safety off and pulling the oh-so-familiar Beretta trigger, the action smooth and the weapon responding in his hand as he began firing. He took the man who was to execute him in the head, dropped a man behind him with a throat shot and scored a third hit between the eyes as another Saudi rushed up with an Uzi in his fists. Somewhere behind him, the deafening roar of Suharto's sawed-off shotgun sounded as the Indonesian reacted. An alarm sounded, and flashing lights filled the anteroom.

Bolan brought his appropriated weapon to track Yusef and pulled the trigger.

Nothing happened. He realized the slide had locked back prematurely. The weapon had only a ten-round magazine, by his mental count. He let it fall, grabbing the submachine gun on its shoulder sling. Bullets filled the air around and above him as the Saudis, scrambling for cover amidst the torn-up office furniture in the anteroom, began returning fire in earnest. Bolan let the weapon go on full-auto as he hosed the enclosed room, careful to keep Suharto behind him and to keep his shots low to avoid the laboratory. The .45 slugs chewed up floor tile and neutral-pattern chairs and sofas as they whipped through the room. The lethal fusillade cleared a path to the laboratory and, more importantly, knocked Yusef down and out of the way. Bolan did not know if the man was hit or had just thrown himself out of the line of fire, but it did not matter. He grabbed a fistful of Suharto's shirt and dragged the Indonesian through the doors to the laboratory, shattering the glass as he smashed his way through. Those within, including Wahid himself, had already hidden themselves behind whatever cover they could find.

"Wahid!" Bolan called.

"Here!" came the doctor's voice. Gunfire split the air. The Saudis were converging in the anteroom and shooting into the lab.

"Cooper!" Suharto called. "We are pinned down!"

"No choice!" Bolan called back. He crawled over to Wahid as automatic and semiautomatic fire from the Saudis smashed into the equipment and the chemicals on the table. Fragments of glass and unidentified liquids splashed down. At least one or two small fires started. Wahid suddenly grew agitated, looking at the laboratory table that was rocking under a hail of bullets.

"No!" he shouted. "No, we will all be killed!" He rose from his spot on the floor.

"No, Wahid!" Bolan called.

The doctor reached for the laboratory table and snatched a vial that sat, untouched, on the scarred and pitted surface. The Saudis never stopped firing, though Bolan could hear Yusef shouting from where he crouched beyond the shattered windows to the anteroom.

Wahid fell. Blood soaked his white lab coat. He looked shocked. He stared at Bolan, who crawled over to stop him from hitting his head on the floor. He held out the vial.

"Theta-Seven," he said. Bolan took the vial cautiously. It looked intact.

"Wahid," he said. "We need to know! Is there a counteragent? Did you learn anything?"

"They…do not know that I…figured it out," Wahid said, speaking English with a British accent.

"Wahid!" Bolan shook the man, not ungently, trying to bring him around as life ebbed out of him. Nearby, Suharto was returning fire as best he could with his reloaded Beretta. The Saudis were beginning to close in.

"Enclosed space…no ventilation…the capsule will…kill those within twenty feet," Wahid said. "It will dissipate…you could…use it…but it would have…killed us…." Bolan looked down at the sample in his hands.

"Wahid, how do we neutralize the weapon? Is it possible?"

"Simple," the dying Wahid said, coughing up blood. "Fire…simple fire…without an explosion…without the energy of a…precursor detonation…you simply…burn it…consume the acid…burn the fumes…"

Bolan leaned closer, trying to hear the doctor over the gunplay. "Wahid?"

The doctor closed his eyes and died, almost peacefully.

"Cooper!" Suharto said urgently. "I am out of ammunition and they are coming!"

Bolan looked down at the vial in his hand. He gauged the distance to the anteroom. He looked at Suharto.

"You are not doing what I think you are doing?" Suharto was aghast.

"Go for the exit." Bolan nodded to the door at the back of the lab, the door they had been unable to reach thanks to the withering Saudi gunfire. "As soon as this hits."

"But…"

"Go!" Bolan said. He pushed to his knees and, like a baseball pitcher, hurled the sample vial as hard as he could through one of the shattered anteroom windows.

He heard Yusef scream as the vial shattered.

The bullets stopped as the Saudis scrambled for their lives. The cloud of toxic gas that was created by the acid hitting the open air quickly enveloped the anteroom. In seconds the security operatives were choking and gasping for breath. Bolan ushered Suharto out the door at the back of the laboratory, but could not help himself. He paused, taking in the carnage in the anteroom, his gaze sweeping across Wahid's prone form to take in those writhing in the outer room. Bolan saw Yusef pull himself up past one of the windows, for only a moment, his face purpling, blood hemorrhaging from his eyes and nose as he screamed. Then he fell back.

The Executioner slammed the laboratory door shut behind him.

13

"You unleashed the chemical!" Suharto said as they ran down the stairs.

"Only in the outer room of the laboratory," Bolan said, hurrying close behind him. "With no explosion to vaporize it and get its chemical reaction moving, it will dissipate. That's what Wahid was trying to tell me. He also told me how to neutralize it."

"How?"

"We burn it," Bolan said. "It can't be an explosion. If I understand him right, the energy of an explosion gets the chemical reaction going, the reaction that turns the vapor cloud loose as nerve gas. Wahid said simple fire will burn the acid and the fumes."

"Fire…" Suharto said.

"Yeah," Bolan returned. It was so simple that it had been overlooked by those seeking a chemical solution of some kind. Wahid, doing his best to keep the Saudis guessing for as long as possible, had evidently figured it out at some point, only to keep working. He had denied the Saudis the solution they were trying to pry from him. Maybe he knew they weren't likely to let him live when they were finished with him. Maybe he just wanted to make things difficult for them. As a chemist intimately familiar with the weapon, he would have known what horror the Saudis had unleashed on the world. Maybe he wanted to make them squirm for as long as possible, perhaps deny them the solution completely if he could. There was no way to know.

The man had given his life and helped Bolan and Suharto on their mission. If the Executioner could help it, the chemist's sacrifice would not be for nothing.

Bolan and Suharto hit the street. A black Mercedes sedan was parked in front of the building, and a single Saudi security agent was emerging from the vehicle. He reached into his coat and withdrew a suppressed pistol of a type Bolan could not identify at that distance. Suharto reacted first, his shotgun coming up, the street cannon cutting loose with both barrels as the Indonesian braced himself against the recoil. The man toppled in a heap on the street next to his car.

"Let's go," Bolan said. Suharto was staring at his handiwork, looking surprised at what had happened. Bolan hooked his shirt and dragged him, taking him past the corpse and shoving him into the Mercedes. The keys were in the ignition. Bolan started the car, slammed the shifter into Drive and put his boot to the floor, taking them screaming from the curb.

As fast as it had happened, it was not fast enough. Perhaps reacting to some sort of alarm at the office building, the Saudis were sending reinforcements. Bolan wondered just how many of them had been devoted to this operation. It seemed as if he had faced a small army at this point. As the Mercedes pulled away and into the busy traffic, two more cars roared up through the stream of vehicles, passing and changing lanes with reckless abandon. The cars were headed straight for Suharto and Bolan.

Either they had seen Bolan and Suharto steal the car, or someone left alive in the office had seen it and radioed to the other vehicles. Either way, the two pursuing cars were intent on catching them.

"We've got to get out of traffic," Bolan said. "Too many people could get hurt!"

"That way." Suharto pointed, and Bolan steered the car through a tire-burning slide around the corner, fishtailing and only barely correcting in time. "The nearest industrial estate. Fewer people. Buildings we can use for cover."

"On my way," Bolan said.

They managed to keep enough distance between the Saudis and their own car to stop the latter from opening fire in traffic, but only barely. Bolan's knuckles were white on the wheel as he pushed himself, hard. He roared up and over curbs, cutting corners as best he could, always avoiding crowds and other cars, trying to maintain the combat stretch with the chasing Saudis. When they reached the industrial estate and found themselves in a dilapidated rail yard, the Saudis no longer had as much traffic to dodge. They closed the gap, their cars homing in like black missiles.

The trio of cars entered the expanse of the rail yard almost abreast, bouncing over the uneven ground and the rails that crisscrossed the yard. Bolan punched the accelerator as hard as he could, and one of the cars fell behind. The other car, however, evidently had a more powerful engine. It stayed with Bolan, coming up on the driver's side. The soldier guided the car left-handed while pulling the submachine gun up, thrusting it out the window in order to clear the space in front of his head. He could not afford to be deafened or blinded by the blast.

Just as the weapon cleared the window, the cunning Saudi driver rammed his car into the driver's side of Bolan's Mercedes. The weapon was slammed between the vehicles, wrenching itself free of Bolan's grasp, pulling his whole right shoulder with it as the weapon dragged him on its shoulder harness. Operating on instinct, Bolan—

struggling with the Mercedes the entire time—pulled his tactical folding knife from his pocket and snapped it open. The serrated blade cut raggedly through the leather strap, freeing him. He wrenched the steering wheel to the other side and broke free of the other car. As he did so, however, the other pursuing vehicle shot forward.

It slammed into the engine compartment of Bolan's vehicle, its nose pushing the passenger side, sending the Mercedes spinning out in the rail yard. Suharto's side air bag deployed with an explosive crack. Bolan rode out the spin, barely waiting when the vehicle came to a halt. He was up and out, shoving the crumpled driver's door open with one foot, filling his fists with the Beretta 93-R and the Desert Eagle. Suharto struggled out of his side of the car.

The lead Mercedes, the one that had tried to pin him against the driver's door, was circling tightly. Bolan brought the big .44 Magnum Desert Eagle up with his left hand, leading the reeling Mercedes just slightly. When the triangular snout of the Desert Eagle blossomed in orange flame, a spiderweb hole appeared in the side window of the Mercedes. The driver lurched forward. The car continued its forward arc, with nothing but deadweight behind the wheel. The men riding inside threw open their doors and jumped out.

"Behind the car!" Bolan called. He and Suharto put their own damaged Mercedes between them and the Saudis. The men in the second Mercedes had suffered badly in the crash. The driver had not moved from his wheel, despite the fact that his air bag, too, had gone off. The two in the backseat, dazed from the impact with Bolan's car, were climbing out as Suharto and Bolan came around to that side of the car. Suharto did not wait; he put a double-barrel shotgun blast through the rear window, tagging one of the Saudis and putting him down for good.

The second man tumbled out of his door and came up with a micro-Uzi in his fists. The 9 mm bullets peppered the side of Bolan's stolen Mercedes. The Executioner slammed himself back against the car, his right arm at full extension. The Beretta 93-R chugged once. The bullet punched through the man's forehead, dropping him in his tracks.

More bullets pinged off the roof of the wrecked Mercedes. Two Saudis, each carrying a compact submachine gun, opened fire, spraying the automobile's frame and shattering what was left of its glass. Bolan and Suharto both hit the deck, then rolled for the dubious protection of the wheels as bullets began to ricochet under the car.

"Suharto," Bolan said. "They're going to home in on us unless we take it to them."

Suharto nodded.

"Ready?"

"Ready," Suharto said grimly.

"On my mark," Bolan said. He waited for the Saudis to pause, reaching to reload their weapons, their training forgotten in their desperate rush to kill.

"Now!" Bolan shouted.

The two men heaved themselves up and around the wrecked Mercedes. Bolan fired both of his guns, while Suharto managed with the tiny Jetfire, his shotgun useless at that range. They drove the Saudis back and Bolan tagged one of them. Suharto managed to wound the other in the leg. The wounded Saudi rolled behind his own Mercedes. Bolan gave chase, moving to stand over him and placing his foot on the man's gun hand before he could bring his micro-Uzi up.

"Stop," Bolan said, the Desert Eagle's giant muzzle pointed straight at the man's head. "It's over."

"It is never over, infidel," the Saudi sneered. He whipped

his body over, bringing his own head in line with the Uzi's barrel as he folded his arm under his chin. The blast was brief and muffled by the proximity of the weapon to flesh and bone. Bolan turned away to avoid the spray.

Suharto was panting as he came up. "Did he…?"

"Yes," Bolan said. "I guess he decided he'd rather go to Allah than answer my questions."

"I feared as much," Suharto said. "The Saudis are known for their fanaticism. There could be many such as he among their ranks."

Bolan looked around, reloading and then holstering his pistols. There were no threats in evidence.

"There are weapons scattered throughout this yard," Bolan said, "and I don't want to leave them for the neighborhood children to play with."

"I will look," Suharto said.

They heard a groan from one of the cars.

The driver of the second Mercedes, who had not moved since the vehicle T-boned Bolan's car, began to stir. His deflated air bag covered the steering wheel beneath him.

"I'm going to question him," Bolan said. "He might know something."

"You will get nothing from him," Suharto said gloomily. "The Saudis are not interested in helping you. Only stopping you and containing this menace they have unleashed."

Bolan knew that was a likely possibility. However, as long as there was some option open to him, he had to take it. "I'm going to try," he said.

"Very well," Suharto said. "I will radio the agency and the local police to let them know what has happened. I will need to speak to my government at length, as well. There will be diplomatic protests on both sides. You are not making my life any easier, Cooper."

"I know," Bolan said. "If it helps, my boss isn't going to like this any better than yours."

"I can see it troubles you," Suharto said, laughing despite himself.

"You," Bolan said, careful to make sure he could see both of the injured Saudi driver's hands. "It's over. Give it up."

"You will get no argument from me," the driver said.

"Care to tell me what you know?"

"I know nothing," the Saudi said. He sounded defeated. "I am only a driver."

"Your team has been operating in the city for what, weeks?"

"Months, actually," the driver said. "Though our ranks have grown recently, as the situation became more urgent."

"Urgent? Urgent how?" Bolan asked.

"I will not tell you," the Saudi said. "Kill me if you must. In truth I think I am dying. Something inside is very wrong. I can feel my bones grind."

Bolan peered inside the driver's compartment. The Saudi held his abdomen tightly. He was not wearing a seat belt and had probably hit the steering wheel, hard.

"Suharto!" Bolan called. "We need an ambulance!"

"I have called!" Suharto shouted from where he was walking back and forth, collecting fallen firearms.

"We are getting medical attention for you," Bolan told the Saudi. "Make no sudden moves."

"I am not likely to," the Saudi said. "You're the American?"

"Yes," Bolan said.

"Why are you here?"

"To stop what's happening," Bolan said truthfully. "To put an end to a danger that originated in your country."

"We should have been on the same side."

"We should have been," Bolan agreed.

"I am a loyal man," the Saudi said. "But I do not always agree with the decisions of those in power. Fighting you…treating all as enemies in trying to contain this threat…that was a mistake."

"It was," Bolan said. "What is your name?"

"Usman," the man replied.

"Are there any more of you?"

"I do not think so," Usman replied, sounding earnest enough through his pain. "I am not sure who might have survived the laboratory. We were called in as the battle raged, and pursued as you left. I have not seen my leader."

"Yusef?"

"He is the second," Usman shook his head. "Yasud Gafar. He leads us here. But I have not seen him, and he did not respond when we called him during the chase."

"Thank you for your honesty," Bolan said. "There may yet be hope."

"For you, perhaps." Usman shook his head weakly. "For me, no. For my family, no. We have failed. Failure is punished severely."

"You could still tell me what else you know," Bolan offered. "We could help you."

"You could…" Usman's voice was weak. "We did…learn something. Before we were recalled to deal with you. Olminsk's men… They were moving on Tugu Muda. We don't know why, but the answer seems obvious. We were about to report it when we received the alert and responded to the laboratory."

"Tugu Muda?"

There was no response.

"Usman?"

Suharto came up, carrying fallen hardware. He offered one to Bolan with a frown. "Here it is, Cooper," he said. "I do not think you should fire it."

The submachine gun had apparently gotten caught in the underside of the Mercedes, likely by the hanging strap after Bolan had cut it free. Something had twisted the barrel out of alignment, leaving it bent. The weapon's receiver was cracked. The firearm had been tough and reliable, but no weapon could have survived a wreck with a full-sized automobile. Bolan took it and regarded it ruefully.

Suharto looked at the dead man. "He did not make it?"

"No," Bolan said.

"I am sorry." He took out his phone. "I will tell them not to hurry."

"We're going to need transportation again," Bolan said. "Tugu Muda."

Suharto's eyes grew wide. "I understand," he said.

"Suharto," Bolan said. "Wahid mentioned fire as the means of destroying the chemicals without detonating them. I have an idea. But we'll need to see what your local resources can provide. There's no time to have something sent by my people."

"I will do what I can," he said.

14

Vasily Radchinko passed through the gates of Lawang Sewu. The Building of a Thousand Doors sat crumbling at the end of Pemuda Street, which was itself a hub of shopping. Radchinko had to admit that for both psychological and physical impact, Olminsk had chosen his target well.

The old Dutch building, which sat within sight—and within rifle distance, more importantly—of the Tugu Muda youth monument, was clearly abandoned. The building, he was given to understand, had once housed a Dutch rail company, and later was prominent in the Second World War when the Javanese fought the Japanese. That was the reason for the Tugu Muda monument, apparently. It commemorated the stand of youthful Indonesians against the Japanese, a battle, Radchinko gathered, where the locals had been victorious.

The man guarding the front gate of Lawang Sewu was one of the pirates they'd hired to assist them. He supposed the original gate guard, a caretaker who sold passes to curious tourists, was dead somewhere.

Radchinko had originally held doubts as to the viability of bringing the Indonesian and Chinese scavengers back to land from their various vessels, but Olminsk had been confident they would come. All it had taken was the promise of money—money Olminsk said he would have in abundance once he proved to the world that the Saudi chemical was as deadly as they knew it to be. They were not much, these pirates, but Radchinko had to admit to himself that he was one of their number and had been for some years now. Gone were the days of the navy; gone were the days of the Soviet Union and even of a proud post-Soviet Russia. This was his fate, and he accepted it. There was a time when he had told himself he would follow Olminsk until one or both of them died. These days, he was not so sure.

He continued to make his way through Lawang Sewu, climbing crumbling steps past signs that undoubtedly told him they were not safe to use. Why such a large and prominent building could be allowed to rot was not lost on Radchinko. He had seen it often enough in the navy. Once-proud ships and submarines left to rust in their berths, falling apart from neglect and from lack of funds. How such an empire could fall would be the most bitter memory of Radchinko's life.

Moss and mold covered many of the surfaces, plaster peeling from red brick. Weeds poked up here and there, through cracks in the stone. Many of the windows were without glass, many of the doors without handles. There were still remnants of the building's past glory, however. There were remarkable stained-glass windows, which time and apathy had not yet diminished. In one alcove he found an old Dutch coat of arms on a stone tablet. A sense of time, and of time passing, crushed in all around him. It was uncomfortable, dwelling on just how much he, and his country, had lost.

He could understand how these things drove Olminsk. At least, he had once understood it. Now, as he moved past caches of the canisters wired to detonators among the rooms of Lawang Sewu, he had his doubts.

Whether the building truly had a thousand doors was a

matter of local lore, he supposed. He was not inclined to count. Certainly there were many. In one of the larger rooms, with several hired Indonesian pirates standing lazy guard with Kalashnikovs, he discovered Chebykin.

The big Russian was happily wiring charges to yellow canisters. Radchinko was struck by just how many of these there were. He did a quick count. The numbers added up fast.

"Kirill," he said to the larger Russian, who was whistling tunelessly, "what are you doing?"

"What I was ordered to do," Chebykin answered in Russian. "I am wiring the detonators to the weapons."

"But…" Radchinko looked around. "This must be all of the canisters."

"All but two," Chebykin said. "Those I hooked up in the jeeps outside, as the Captain ordered."

"But Kirill," Radchinko said, "if these are all the canisters, what is the point of detonating them?"

"To see them go!" Chebykin smiled. Then he looked to Radchinko, confused. "Why?"

"Don't you understand?" Radchinko said. "This was supposed to be a demonstration. We were going to show the world what the weapon can do, so that the Captain could sell the chemical at a profit. How can we sell what we have destroyed?"

"I don't know, and I don't care," Chebykin said. "The Captain says make them ready to blow up, I make them ready to blow up. He has taken good care of us until now."

"Yes," Radchinko said. "Until now." He thought for a moment, looking around. The sentries regarded him without curiosity, cigarettes dangling lazily from their mouths. He doubted they would have understood a single word of the conversation, any more than Radchinko understood Indonesian or Javanese. "Continue with your work, then."

"I was going to," Chebykin said crossly. "Leave me be."

Radchinko swallowed a curse. This was not the time to argue with the big Russian, and he was not confident he could subdue the man without being forced to kill him. Swearing to himself, he hunted through the crumbling corridors of Lawang Sewu.

Eventually Radchinko found Olminsk on the landing of one of the building's towers, where he was setting up the rifle. The scoped Remington, an American sniper weapon Radchinko had himself acquired from an illicit arms market in Jakarta, was resting against the wall beneath the window. Through the window Radchinko could see Tugu Muda.

"Ah, Vasily," Olminsk said, picking up the weapon and sighting through the Remington's scope. "It is good you are here. Will you take the honors of wielding the rifle?"

"To what purpose?" Radchinko asked.

"The plan is a simple one," Olminsk said, sounding distracted as he watched the monument and the street around it. "Timofei will lead the detachment with the two trucks. They will take up positions outside Tugu Muda. One of us will use the rifle here, for cover, to take out the police as they approach. And before that becomes an issue, our people will begin firing."

"Firing? You intend simply to gun down civilians?"

"We are all civilians, Vasily," Olminsk said. "But it is necessary. It will draw the attention of the police and of the media, such as it is here. When we have a crowd gathered, we will detonate the chemicals. Among the pirates who will assist Timofei are a pair with camera phones. They will record the effects and transmit them to me."

"To what purpose?" Radchinko asked again. "I have seen Kirill downstairs. He is wiring up the remaining chemical, all of it! What will we sell? What good is your demonstration?"

"Things have progressed," Olminsk said. He set the rifle down and turned to face Radchinko. "I have been in communication with a group who heard my first transmission. Even without the demonstration aboard the cruise ship, they were interested. We have worked a deal. I require the video in order to show them proof. In truth I think perhaps they simply enjoy watching death, too. But that is not important."

"What sort of deal? Who are these people?"

"An al Qaeda splinter group," Olminsk admitted. "Dangerous people, yes. And quite mad. But also rich. They have wired a substantial sum to my private account. When the job is done, they will wire the second half. It will be enough for me to retire. Enough for all of us to retire. And when this group takes credit for the destruction, as they desire to do, I will have struck a blow against the West by helping them. I have decided this is sufficient."

"Why would they do this? What do they ask you to do?"

"To destroy the city," Olminsk said. "It is no small thing, to wipe out a city of one and a half million people. But using all of the Saudi chemical, together, wired to explode at the same time, should produce a chemical cloud of sufficient size. It may not kill *everyone,* but it will kill enough. Semarang will die."

"But…why?" Radchinko was horrified.

"Why not?" Olminsk said. "What have these people done for us?"

"But you have made a life here," Radchinko said. "Your business interests. These last few years…"

"Years spent as a filthy pirate? As a criminal?" Olminsk said bitterly. "Why would that hold anything but dishonor for me? Vasily, I thought you understood. We have been merely biding our time these last years, doing what was necessary to build a fortune. I have always remained loyal to Mother Russia. I thought you had, too."

"Of course I have!" Radchinko said. "But to kill an entire city…for what?"

"For money," Olminsk said. "Enough money so that I need never work again. I can leave all this behind. Tell me it does not appeal to you, Vasily. Did you truly enjoy being a pirate? Being seagoing scum? Associating with the sorts of men I now hire to do our bidding? Did you enjoy the company of people like Tranh and his murderers, child molesters and rapists?"

"We do not know that this plan can succeed," Radchinko said. "What if we are found? The Saudi security people have—"

"Have what?" Olminsk said. "They cannot stop us."

"But we think they killed Grigori, and Ilya," Radchinko said. "They are following us. They know who we are, what we are trying to do."

"They know more than I would like, but less than you think," Olminsk said. "I have set a trap for them. Leonid waits for them even now, and when he is done, he will erase them from existence. As well as any evidence we may have left in storage that could ever tie any of this to us."

"How?"

"Does it matter?" Olminsk said. "You are not likely to see him again, but then, that has always been Leonid's secret desire. He has always wished for death."

"I don't understand, Captain."

"Nor do you need to!" Olminsk said angrily. "Simply follow my orders!"

"But, Captain," Radchinko said, edging away from his fellow Russian. "This is not what I signed on for. I was loyal to you. There was money in it. You were a reason-able businessman. But this is mass murder. I cannot do it."

"You would betray me? After everything we have been through together? You, Vasily, my most loyal subordi-nate?"

"I have my limits, Captain," Vasily said. "You have crossed them."

"That is most unfortunate," Olminsk said. The Stechkin machine pistol that appeared in his hand had been a faithful companion for many years. Vasily saw the move coming and ducked aside. The burst of Makarov rounds sprayed the peeling bricks behind him and raised a cloud of fragments as Olminsk emptied the magazine.

Radchinko ran. As he did so he fumbled with his own pistol, an American-made Colt 1911. He snapped off a shot as he ran, the heavy .45 slug chipping brick as it struck somewhere wide of his pursuer. He stumbled down a flight of stairs, tripped and landed flat on his face on the weed-cracked stone, turning just in time to see Olminsk standing over him. The barrel of the Stechkin seemed to open wide, an endless chasm swallowing all that he had ever been and all that he would ever be.

"Comrade," Radchinko said, pushing the Colt away from him on the stone. He raised his hands, palms up, as he lay on his back facing his former Captain. "Please. After all these years…do not kill me. I will not interfere in your plans. Allow me to leave."

"Do you think," Olminsk said, and for the first time Radchinko recognized the light of madness in the man's eyes, "that your life means anything to me?"

"We have been crew mates for years, comrade."

"You were my subordinate," Olminsk said, "and you never stopped being such. You are just a tool, Radchinko.

You, like poor, stupid, brutal Grigori. You, like poor, dumb, gun-crazy Ilya. You, like poor, depressed Leonid, who was happy to give his life if only it meant his pain stopped. You, like that idiot Timofei, who will give his life at Tugu Muda and does not even know it. You are a means to an end. I will have my revenge, and I will live out my days in luxury. No part of my old life will follow me to the new!"

"Captain, wait!"

Olminsk had reloaded the Stechkin. He aimed it and emptied its twenty-round magazine, laughing as he did so.

The gunfire echoed through the empty, crumbling hallways of Lawang Sewu. Olminsk was again reloading the Stechkin when Chebykin came lumbering into the corridor.

"Captain?"

"Vasily disappoints me," Olminsk said. He held the Russian-made machine pistol casually. He made no attempt to bring it on target, but such a weapon was lethal in the close quarters of the corridor. Both men knew it.

"Sir?"

"He was plotting to betray us," Olminsk said. "His nerve had gone soft."

Chebykin grunted. "I never liked him."

Olminsk looked at him. "You did not?"

"He was always…thinking. Too much. Thought he was smarter than everyone else."

"An interesting perspective," Olminsk said. He holstered the Stechkin at his side.

"Orders, Captain?"

"Have you finished wiring the canisters?"

"Yes," he said. "Here is the detonator. The code is nine-nine-eight."

"Good work," Olminsk said. "Would you like to join Timofei in the assault outside?"

"I could use the action," Chebykin said. "It would feel good to fire a few rounds for a change."

"Then see Timofei and ride with the trucks out to the youth monument," Olminsk instructed. "And, Kirill?"

"Yes, Captain?"

"Be sure to wear your gas mask, when the canisters detonate. I would not wish to lose you."

"No, sir." Kirill smiled. "Of course not."

15

Suharto brought the old vehicle to a halt. He looked up at the building, so imposing against the bright blue sky. Then he turned to Bolan. "That is it," he said.

"Lawang Sewu," Bolan said, repeating the name Suharto had given him. They were still quite some distance away. Bolan had insisted they not get any closer.

"The Building of a Thousand Doors," Suharto said. "And within sight of it, Tugu Muda, the youth monument."

"Just the sort of public place Olminsk would choose for a demonstration of the weapon," Bolan mused.

"If that is so, why are we here?" Suharto nodded up to the crumbling building, no less beautiful for its state of disrepair and neglect.

"Because any tactical assessment of the situation would make this building the perfect staging area," Bolan said. "It has a good view of the monument and more than enough space to conceal troops. Not to mention the Theta-Seven."

"What do you think he will do?"

"Something public. Something vicious." Bolan assessed it. "We've got to get in there and get started *now*." He looked Suharto in the eye. "You understand what to do?"

"I do."

"They checked you out on the thing?"

"As thoroughly as was possible in the time available. Do not worry. I know what to do."

"All right." He looked up at the building. "Do you think it will survive?"

"Brick and plaster," Suharto said. "I imagine much of the building's materials traveled here with the Dutch as ballast. Of course, I could be wrong. I never was very good with historical details."

Bolan raised an eyebrow.

"It will be okay," Suharto said. "Much better than the alternative."

"All right, then," Bolan said. "Wait here until I've had a chance to clear a path for you. Then follow. Remember, they could be moving around in there. I can't guarantee that I'll be able to intercept them all. You might stumble across one, or more than one."

"I know," Suharto said. "I was able to get this." He held up a Smith & Wesson 9 mm automatic. "Slightly better than my little pocket auto. And not as difficult to wield as the shotgun."

"Do what you've got to," Bolan said. "But make it count. When you see the canisters, you'll know how to handle it."

"I will," Suharto said.

"Give me a five-minute head start," Bolan instructed. "Then come in."

"Five minutes," Suharto said. "I understand."

Bolan made his way into the Lawang Sewu property. He knew the front gate was manned, so he opted to make his infiltration from the back of the property. It was easy enough to get past the rusting fence and crumbling gates. He found a likely point of entry and tried the door, easing it open to avoid making too much noise.

He found himself in a long, tiled corridor. There were, as the tourist literature suggested, many doors. There was one every few steps, it seemed, as he crept deeper into

Lawang Sewu. He watched for sentries and kept an ear out for other signs of activity as he moved.

He had discarded his tunic and wore his boots, khaki pants and a black T-shirt with his leather combat harness over it. The Beretta 93-R and its magazines rode securely under his arms, while the Desert Eagle was on his hip in its holster. He was counting on the Beretta and its Kissinger-custom suppressor to help him make his way quietly through the building, eliminating those he encountered.

The troops he was likely to come up against would be Olminsk's. It was very likely that all the men or women Bolan found working for the Russian captain would be pirates of some order or other. Well, that was all right. Hal Brognola had originally sent the Executioner to deal with a pirate problem, and a pirate problem was exactly what he had been eliminating in Indonesia ever since. There was no reason not to make as clean a sweep of it as possible.

Bolan smelled the sentry before he heard him or saw him. The scent of clove cigarettes drifted down from the crumbling stairwell. Bolan flattened himself against the nearest wall and waited.

The sentry on patrol carried an ancient M-16 in his hands, most of its finish worn off, the triangular hand-guards dating it perhaps to the Vietnam era.

The sentry turned, shock and surprise registering on his face and raised his rifle. Bolan struck with an overhand thrust, the spear-point blade lodging deep in the man's sub-clavian artery. He went down gurgling, unable to scream as Bolan covered his mouth with one hand. Once he was safely out of the action, Bolan popped open the M-16 and removed the bolt, tossing it down the other end of the hallway. The echoes of its fall did not draw any other sentries, which is what Bolan had wanted to test.

Bolan cleaned his knife on the man's shirt and re-sheathed the blade.

The Executioner continued to infiltrate the building.

Another sentry, this one more alert than the smoker, was waiting at the end of the next corridor. Bolan moved as quietly and efficiently as he could, drawing the Beretta 93-R. When the man spotted him, he put a single sup-pressed round through the man's head. He fell like a sack of gravel, folding in on himself almost without a sound. Bolan heard a second man coming, perhaps to check on his friend, or perhaps just on patrol. He froze, counting on the dim hallway and his own lack of movement to confuse the approaching hostile just long enough.

The gambit worked. The man approaching was another Indonesian, more than likely another hired pirate gun. He had a revolver thrust in his belt and was listening to a digital music player. Whatever he was listening to was loud enough to sound like so much noise, to Bolan's ears, but it had also deafened the man. He almost blundered straight into the Executioner, stopping mere feet away when he realized he was not alone in the corridor.

The man's jaw dropped as his brain processed what he was seeing. As the pirate grabbed for his revolver, Bolan put the suppressed muzzle of the Beretta to his forehead and pulled the trigger. He was dead even before gravity started to pull on the upright corpse.

Leaving the bodies behind him, Bolan eventually found the hall he had been searching for, the space he had known must be in Lawang Sewu. Once he was staring at them—a sea of yellow canisters, each with an electronic detona-tor affixed—he was almost taken aback by just how many Olminsk had managed to capture and move. The hall was filled with them, and there was no doubt in Bolan's mind that the explosions awaiting each were more than enough to produce a toxic cloud of incredible size. Based on the intelligence the Farm had provided, this number of canisters would be enough to poison almost the entire city.

He heard approaching footsteps and raised the Beretta.

"Beautiful, is it not?" Vadim Olminsk, looking older but unmistakable compared to his file photo, stepped into view. He was dressed in loose clothing in the local Javanese style. He held an electronic detonator in his hand.

"Place the detonator on the floor," Bolan said, the Beretta trained on Olminsk's head.

"No," Olminsk said. "Place your gun on the floor."

"Not going to happen."

"Then it is a standoff." Olminsk laughed. "At least until I decide I wish to die. And then I push this button and the entire city of Semarang dies with me."

"You don't have to do that," Bolan said, trying to reason with the man. "It won't solve anything. You won't get your money."

"I already have money," Olminsk said. "Though I will get more once these detonate."

"You won't be able to spend it if you go up with them."

"No," Olminsk said. "That would be inconvenient." Suddenly his arm was up, pointing what looked like a Stechkin machine pistol at the rows of canisters. "Of course there is another possibility," he said, laughing. "And that is if a stray bullet, or a not-so-stray bullet, punctures one of these. Then we die, quite horribly."

"I have seen it," Bolan said.

"Have you, now?" Olminsk waved the Stechkin casually. The whole time, he kept the electronic detonator in his other hand, his thumb poised over the keypad. "Horrible, was it?"

"It wasn't pretty."

"So the Saudis warned me, the two whom I had tortured, the two I found guarding the stuff when I took it," Olminsk said. His eyes narrowed. "What are you doing here?"

Bolan shrugged. "This is where the trail led. This is where it ends."

"Led," Olminsk repeated. "You do not mean to tell me…surely it was not you aboard the *Duyfken Ster?*"

Bolan said nothing.

"It *was!*" Olminsk sounded surprised, pleased and shocked all at the same time. "How large was your team?"

Bolan still did not respond.

"All right," Olminsk said. "You will tell me nothing. Fine. Shall I explain to you why I hope to do this terrible thing? Perhaps a confession in my final hours? You do intend to kill me, do you not?"

"I don't care why you're doing what you're doing," Bolan said. "I'm only here to stop you. If that means killing you, so be it."

"How very straightforward of you," Olminsk said. "You will not be offended, I hope, if I am not terribly cooperative?"

Bolan did not respond.

"Do you have any idea," he said, "what it means to have everything you have ever loved, everything you have ever cared about, ripped from you? Do you know what that can do to a man's mind? What it can drive a man to do, to be capable of?"

"As a matter of fact," Bolan said, "I do."

"Then we are not so different."

"We are nothing alike," Bolan said. "You kill the innocent to take what you want. I harvest the guilty. You prey. I protect."

"That is surprisingly poetic," Olminsk said. "I will remember you, long after you are dead."

"I don't see you living a long and fruitful life," Bolan said.

"No? Perhaps not. But I shall outlive you."

"Doubtful."

Olminsk appeared to think about that. The light of insanity played across his eyes. "I think perhaps you may be right. Very well," he said. Holding the detonator in his left hand, he made a show of placing the Stechkin in his belt. Then he withdrew a small two-way radio from his pocket. He spoke a single word of Russian into the radio.

"What did you just do?" Bolan asked.

"It has begun," he said. "Even now, my men will be riding to attack Tugu Muda. The killing will be legendary! They will strike whomever is at hand. They will draw a crowd. They will create an incident the likes of which this city has never seen. And then, when they are all watching, when they all have time to fear, they will see their deaths in the explosions here, and they will know in their last moments that they were powerless to stop it! Let them experience what I have! Let them lose what I have lost!"

He broke and ran.

Bolan pursued. He almost walked into a hail of bullets as Olminsk unloaded the Stechkin at him. The Russian machine pistol sprayed the corridor outside the canister hall, sending Bolan ducking back into the hall for cover. He heard Olminsk's pistol run dry and managed return fire of his own from around the doorway, sending Olminsk running around the opposite corner. Bolan gave chase.

There were a hundred places in Lawang Sewu where the Russian captain could hide. Bolan could not afford to lose him. He had to have that detonator. If the Russian managed to get to a safe distance and trigger his charges—Bolan was gambling that Olminsk was not suicidal—it was over for the city of Semarang, and for one and a half million people.

The gunfire brought two of Olminsk's men running. The pirates, both of them locals, took up positions at the end of the corridor opposite Bolan. Both had Kalashnikovs. The hollow metal rattle of the weapons, so distinctively burned into Bolan's memory, filled the brick and plaster hallway as the bullets drove Bolan into the cover of a doorway. He returned fire blindly, trying to push the gunners back. As he did so, he pushed off, throwing himself down the corridor as the Beretta spat jacketed destruction.

Bolan hurled himself through the open doorway at the end of the corridor. He landed heavily on his side, grunting as shock reverberated through his ribs. The two pirates looked down in horror and began to swing their rifles his way. The Executioner tracked first left, then right, dropping tri-bursts from the machine pistol into each man's center of mass. They fell.

In the silence that followed, Bolan could hear footfalls. Olminsk was on the run and climbing a nearby set of stone steps. He went after the Russian, wary of ambush, reloading the Beretta with a fresh 20-round magazine as he did so.

The tower into which Bolan followed Olminsk was a natural fatal funnel. Both men knew it. Olminsk began firing his Stechkin, spraying the steps below him as he continued to run.

"Olminsk!" Bolan shouted. "There's nowhere to go! You're trapped up there!"

The Russian answered with another magazine-emptying spray from the Stechkin.

"Call it off!" Bolan called again. "There's still time to stop the killing! You can walk away from this alive!"

"And spend the rest of my life in prison?" Olminsk shouted back. "Perhaps they will merely execute me when they get around to it. No, American, I think the city of Semarang dies tonight!"

Bolan froze.

Through the nearest window opening, Bolan started to hear distant gunfire. He heard the squeal of tires as vehicles were brought to screeching halts. Ignoring Olminsk at the top of the tower steps for a moment, he went to the window and peered out. He could just make out Tugu Muda. Two vehicles had parked on opposite sides of the monument. Armed men were stepping out of the vehicles, firing as they climbed out. They were shooting into the passing traffic!

Bolan turned, only to be met with another firestorm from the Russian's automatic weapon. The burst was followed by Olminsk himself, who used it for cover as he dashed down the steps and tried to shove past Bolan.

The veteran sea captain almost made it. He slammed past Bolan and, not a small man himself, managed to put the big American off balance. He had emptied his magazine in his zeal to drive Bolan out of the way, however. As he ran the way they'd both come, Bolan snapped off a single round. The bullet struck Olminsk in the leg, toppling him. Before Bolan could reach him, however, he had thrown himself down the next flight of stairs, headed toward the canister hall.

The soldier caught up with the Russian just as Olminsk was crawling into the hall bearing the Theta-Seven tanks. Bolan slowed, careful of the Russian's weapon, but Olminsk had thrown down the Stechkin. He had apparently run out of ammunition. He paused, on his knees, near the closest of the canisters.

He was frantically pressing a code into the electronic detonator he carried.

"Olminsk! No!" Bolan reached him and tore the detonator from his hand, slamming an elbow across the Russian's face. Olminsk swore again in his native tongue.

"It does not work!" he screamed. "All for nothing!"

Bolan slammed a boot into Olminsk's gut, doubling him over. He kicked the Stechkin away just to be safe. Olminsk curled into a ball, coughing.

The detonator was blinking. A code had been entered into it.

The electronic devices on the canisters still showed green LEDs.

Bolan exhaled. Something had gone wrong. Some crucial component in the detonator had been faulty, apparently. He popped open the case at the rear of the device and slipped out the batteries. For a fraction of a second he wondered if that act might set off the canisters in some way, but logically there was no way for it to do so. The Theta-Seven remained undetonated.

They had stopped this crisis. But he could still hear distant gunfire from Tugu Muda. The slaughter Olminsk had planned for the youth monument—evidently as a diversion or a precursor to what he planned to do in Lawang Sewu—had only started. He started for the door.

A single pirate stood there, his cigarette falling from his mouth in surprise. He shouted something in Indonesian and brought his Kalashnikov up.

Bolan pushed the Beretta to full extension and pulled the trigger.

The Kalashnikov fired.

Bolan's 9 mm bullet took the pirate in the face, folding him over.

The Kalashnikov bullet, its trajectory a one-in-a-million shot, burned through the air across the hall and struck the relatively fragile nozzle of one of the yellow Saudi canisters.

As if in slow motion, Bolan turned to watch the canister nozzle rupture. Deadly Theta-Seven acid began spraying from the nozzle.

"Cooper!" Suharto shouted. "Down!"

Mack Bolan threw himself to the floor and covered his head with his arms. Above him, the air turned to hell-hot fury, scorching Bolan's back and almost suffocating him.

Suharto stood in the doorway, the ominous muzzle of the recently appropriated M2A1-7 flamethrower pointing before him. The heavy Vietnam-era weapon was strapped awkwardly to his back. A tongue of flame reached out across the room and ignited the spraying acid, turning it into a jet of blue fire that scorched the canister next to it.

"Cooper!" Suharto shouted above the noise. "You must get out of this room! Come to me!"

Bolan needed no prodding. He crawled out from under the orange jet of liquid fire and made his way to the doorway where Suharto stood. The Indonesian intelligence operative was drenched in sweat. His face was a mask of grim determination as he waved the flamethrower's shrouded nozzle from side to side, touching each canister with the hellstorm it generated. Each time the flame from the M2A1-7—or from one of the already burning canisters—touched another canister, it burst the nozzle mechanism and set the contents aflame. These in turn jumped to the next canister.

Bolan and Suharto backed away as the fire roiled like Dante's vision of the lowest circles. Suharto did not stop until he had successfully burned each and every tank, the cleansing flame ending the threat of the acid before it could create the deadly fumes that would poison those nearby.

"Come on," Bolan shouted over the noise of the inferno. "We have to get Olminsk and then get to Tugu Muda!"

"Cooper!" Suharto pointed.

Olminsk was gone.

16

The big Caucasian, most likely a Russian, held the long-barreled, bipod equipped RPK in his fists as if it were a toy. He had a drum magazine affixed and was laughing as he sprayed the weapon into the surrounding cars. The police scrambled and returned fire, but they were out-gunned. They had handguns, for the most part, and were shooting from the cover of their engine blocks as the big man chopped away at the vehicles.

Local law enforcement had quickly erected a series of roadblocks around Tugu Muda, after the initial attacks at the youth monument. The pirates had started with two vehicles and plenty of heavy weaponry. They had lobbed a few grenades at the police cars, but they had not deto-nated. Whatever surplus hardware Olminsk had found for them was not without problems, it seemed.

Not long after the police arrived, the pirates managed to overtake two of the nearest police vehicles. They killed the officers and appropriated their cars, complete with bullet-flattened tires, to use as cover. They had lost a man in the process, but there were at least a dozen men still active—two Caucasians who were likely Russians, and ten locals.

"Suharto," Bolan said, lowering his rifle. He had been using the scope to watch the action below and assess the tactical possibilities. He turned to the Indonesian as they stood in the tower in Lawang Sewu. "Are you sure you can get close enough?"

"I am sure," Suharto said. "Do not worry, Cooper. As I said, I am in this until the end."

Bolan sighted once more through the Remington 700 he had found in the tower. Through its powerful scope he could see a yellow Theta-Seven canister in the back of each of the two vehicles the pirates had driven to Tugu Muda. The presence of the weapon indicated a keen tactical mind in Olminsk. Obviously the original plan had called for someone in Lawang Sewu to cover the pirates at the monument, running sniper interference for them as they drew public attention. It was an effective plan. Once enough attention was fixed on the youth monument, Olminsk would have been able to detonate the canisters in the old building, probably from a safe location. It was likely he had intended to kill off many if not all of his allies, too. Bolan could see no way for the pirates to make it out alive, given the volume of Theta-Seven Olminsk had planned to set loose on Semarang. Most of the pirates would never know that their leader had plotted to betray them.

They had searched the grounds immediately after Olminsk's escape, but the Russian captain was nowhere to be found. As much as it galled Bolan to let the man go, he had bigger problems to handle. While the major threat to the city had been neutralized, many lives still hinged on stopping the public demonstration at the youth monument. The pirates showed no inclination to stop what they were doing even in Olminsk's absence. No doubt they had their orders and had no idea the Russian captain was now missing in action.

Reaching into his war bag, Bolan produced four small cylinders. They were Kissinger-special phosphorous grenades. "These burn hot and bright, as soon as they hit the air. They should be enough to destroy the chemicals in the jeeps."

"You will clear a path for me?" Suharto asked.

"Think of me as your guardian angel," Bolan said.

Suharto left. Bolan had to admit that the intelligence operative had shown a lot of steel in a fight he'd been drafted into by a combination of circumstance and simple bureaucracy. There was no way the man could have known the kind of war he was signing up to fight before the first bullets began to fly. He had risen to the challenge. Pramana Suharto had more than earned his respect as a fellow warrior on this worldwide battleground.

Bolan settled himself into the tower window, using the chair that had been brought by Olminsk or one of his pirates. Resting the Remington on the chipped and flaking plaster of the window opening, he brought it to his shoulder and sought the cheek weld that was so familiar to him. He drew in a deep breath, let out half of it, and let the total calm of long-distance shooting claim his body and mind. The entire universe shrank to the crosshairs, his window into it was the scope. In the powerfully magnified image, he placed the killing cross over the shoulder blades of one of the pirates who was firing a Kalashnikov from what he believed was the cover of one of the engine blocks.

Bolan let the rifle fire on its own, when it was ready. It bucked against his shoulder, the .308-caliber bullet rocketing through the target. The pirate was dead before his body bounced against the frame of the vehicle. Bolan ejected the spent round and jacked another into the chamber.

He tracked to the next target. The pirates were all at least partially concealed, using the vehicles for cover as they traded fire with the local police. The man Bolan truly wanted was the big Russian with the RPK. Each time he tried to draw a bead on the lumbering man, however, he lost the shot, as the gunner moved in and out between the vehicles.

Bolan looked past the scope, watching as Suharto slowly made his way past the police cordon. The Indonesian stopped and argued, briefly, with one of the police, possibly a field commander or just a ranking officer. Then he was on his way again, skirting the worst of the shooting, using the ring of vehicles and hastily erected wooden roadblocks to mask his progress as he worked his way around.

Media trucks were being held back at the farthest perimeter of the cordon. The reporters and camera operators swarmed about, trying to get decent shots.

Suharto was reaching a critical juncture. He was hiding behind a bullet-pocked police minivan. Within sprinting distance was one of the pirate jeeps concealing three shooters. The Theta-Seven canister was sheltered in the cargo bed of the vehicle, and so far had not been punctured by a bullet. That was definitely a risk, and while the gas would not go far enough to endanger those not on the immediate scene, it was likely that many of the police responders would be killed by the toxic fumes created if one or both of the canisters were punctured.

Bolan suspected that the pirates had only the vaguest notion of the dangers of the Saudi acid. He had caught a glimpse, briefly, of one pirate with a gas mask clipped to his belt. According to the data provided by Brognola and Stony Man, the fumes would eat through a gas-mask filter as if it were not there. Having seen the painful death that awaited those exposed to the chemical, Bolan did not wish it on anyone—not even the murderous bastards shooting in the shadow of Tugu Muda.

The crosshairs settled on one of the three men trying to aim at Suharto. Bolan went through his firing mantra again, clearing his mind, taking a breath and then letting half of it out. The rifle fired, the trigger breaking when it was ready. The pirate, perhaps experiencing a moment's precognition, looked up with the dread that all doomed men feel when death comes calling. He died instantly when the jacketed slug punched through his skull.

Bolan worked the Remington's bolt and reacquired his sight picture. The two survivors realized that a threat greater than the police was now presenting itself. They started to look up and around, pointing their rifles this way and that, becoming frantic as they tried to see from where death was hunting them. One of them popped up just a bit too far from the cover of the vehicle and was felled by a police bullet.

The third man looked up and, from Bolan's magnified point of view, straight into the Executioner's eyes. Through the scope, the soldier could see his prey saying something. Whatever the man's last words, they were lost when Bolan's bullet punched a hole through his face, snapping his head back and launching him into oblivion.

Suharto was on the move, the police doing what they could to cover him. The RPK gunner and the other Russian had taken shelter inside the other jeep, while those pirates still mobile were running in confusion around it. Two more were dropped by police shooters as Bolan watched.

The flash was bright, even at this distance. It looked to Bolan like Suharto used two of the phosphorous grenades, just as the soldier had instructed him. There was one flash, then another a microsecond later, the retina-searing bursts overlapping. The jeep was quickly ablaze in chemical fire. A moment later, Bolan could see the canister in the back of the jeep blow its seal. The toxic acid spewed forth as a gout of flame, the fire consuming the deadly chemical as it leaped forward from its pressurized prison. Suharto left the burning vehicle behind and ran for the second.

The second truck almost struck the Indonesian. The two Russians had started the bullet-riddled vehicle. On rims sparking through torn, twisted, flattened radials, it lurched forward, slamming into the burning wreckage of its counterpart. Suharto dodged aside. Bolan, watching and trying to get a shot at the driver, was thwarted by the vehicle's proximity to its twin. The other burning wreckage blocked the jeep's spiderwebbed windshield, preventing him from taking the shot. The truck was moving out of effective range as the angle became too great. It looked as if it was heading right back for Bolan and Lawang Sewu.

Suharto wasn't done yet. As Bolan watched, he ran after the jeep. Bullets pocked the paving around Tugu Muda. The police used the distraction to take out the remainder of the pirates, while some tried to shoot at the moving jeep. Suharto, at great risk to himself from both the police gunfire and from the two men in the moving vehicle, stayed with the limping truck. The RPK gunner blitzed the police cordon with his weapon, spraying lethal 7.62 mm fire from the drum magazine. When the damaged jeep made its way through the cordon in a shower of sparks from the rims, Suharto managed to get just close enough to pitch in his two remaining phosphorus cylinders.

The grenades went off almost simultaneously. The explosion was followed by the rupture of the Theta-Seven canister, adding its own tongue of fire to the conflagration in the rear of the truck. As the burning vehicle smashed its way past the gate to Lawang Sewu, the two men inside ran screaming from it, chased by police gunfire and a running Suharto's own 9 mm bullets.

They were in the building.

Bolan quickly removed the Remington's bolt and pocketed it, to prevent the weapon from being recovered and used against him. Then, with his Desert Eagle in his fist, he left the tower, determined to hunt the two fugitive pirates until he brought them to ground. Somewhere below him, Suharto would be driving the two men to him. With the Theta-Seven threat ended, hopefully for good, it was time to bring to a close this particular chapter in the book of international terrorism and mayhem.

Bolan hurried down from the tower and took the nearest corridor to the next landing. He almost ran into the big RPK gunner as the man rounded the corner. Screaming in Russian, the big man straight-armed Bolan, the savage force of the blow staggering the Executioner. The Russian used his RPK like a club, hammering Bolan with the wooden stock, knocking him senseless with a powerful thrust to the head. Then he dropped the weapon—empty or simply forgotten—and wrapped his fingers around Bolan's neck.

The soldier saw a bright flash and began to lose consciousness. Darkness started to encroach on the edges of his vision. If he lost it, if he went out now, he knew he would never wake up. The Russian was going to kill him with nothing but bare hands.

He heard a gunshot. The Russian's eyes grew wide and he tried to reach back behind his shoulder blades. Throwing Bolan aside like a broken doll, he turned. Suharto stood there with his pistol, looking horrified that the bullet had not brought down the giant. He fired twice more as the big Russian closed in on him. The larger man screamed wordlessly and caught Suharto in a bone-crushing bear hug, trying to squeeze the life out of the smaller man with nothing but muscle and rage. Suharto shrieked, gagged and then slumped, as the big man brought his mammoth arms together.

Bolan staggered to his feet, trying to clear his head. He had lost the Desert Eagle and, with his vision blurry, could not locate it. He drew the Beretta 93-R with a shaking hand, trying to line up a shot on the big Russian. The Russian, perhaps sensing the threat, or perhaps catching some glimpse of Bolan from the corner of his eye, turned to put the helpless Suharto between the Russian and Bolan's gun. The soldier dropped the muzzle of the weapon.

"I have you now!" the Russian said, blood flecking his lips. "Put down your gun, or I will kill him!"

Bolan's sight was clearing. His hand grew firm on the butt of the Beretta. "Let him go," he said.

The Russian squeezed tighter.

Bolan aimed low, putting a three-round burst through the Russian's kneecap. The man bellowed and collapsed, dropping Suharto, and clutched at the ruins of his knee.

"Down!" Bolan ordered. "On the ground! Get down!"

"You will not stop me," the Russian growled. "I am Kirill Chebykin. I am the fist of Mother Russia. I am loyal. I am *strong*." The big Russian spoke the words almost as a mantra.

With speed Bolan would have thought impossible in a man wounded so badly, Chebykin shot to one foot with a thrust from his good leg. His shattered knee and the leg below it dragged uselessly as he threw himself onto Bolan.

The Executioner triggered the Beretta again. The Russian's weight crushed down on him, his large hands seeking purchase on Bolan's head, his fingers poking and clawing. Bolan tucked his head against his chest, protecting his vulnerable eyes, as the Russian groped and prodded, trying to blind him or choke him.

The Executioner emptied the Beretta into the raging

giant, the bullets tearing through his chest. At long last one of the hollow points found the man's heart. He died abruptly, after so much abuse, his last breath sighing from his lungs in an almost anticlimactic death rattle. He stopped clawing and gouging and became three hundred pounds of deadweight on top of Bolan.

The Executioner crawled out from under the bloody, bullet-riddled corpse.

"Suharto," he called. "You all right?"

"There…there are two," Suharto said, gasping for breath. "The other one is here somewhere."

Bolan crawled over to where Suharto lay on the moldy floor. "Are you hurt?"

"There may be…something internal," Suharto wheezed. "It may only be cracked ribs. But I hurt very badly. It is difficult to breathe."

"Stay here," Bolan told him. "Do you have rounds left?"

"I am not sure," Suharto said. "I have lost my gun."

Bolan found his own Desert Eagle and holstered it, then retrieved Suharto's fallen Smith & Wesson. He checked it, loaded a spare magazine from those Suharto kept on him, and placed the weapon in Suharto's hand.

"Stay here," he repeated. "Keep an eye out. Can you sit up?"

"I can try," Suharto said. "Before they came in, I called the police forces. They have surrounded the building. They claim they will wait for my signal."

"So we have him," Bolan said. "Somewhere in here."

"Very likely."

Bolan helped him prop himself up against the wall of the corridor. "I'm going to search the building, then. If you see him, don't wait. Just shoot him. Near as I can tell this is the last of them, unless any of them survived the fight outside."

"Cooper."

"Yeah?"

"I will be very glad when we are done with this work." Suharto managed a white-toothed grin. "Working with you is very bad for my health. I need a vacation."

"That makes two of us," Bolan said.

17

Mack Bolan stalked through Lawang Sewu, once more hunting a man. With his flashlight and the Desert Eagle in his hands, he searched out every darkened corner, the light strobing briefly whenever he needed a moment's illumination. Low-light tactics with pistol and flashlight were simple enough—strobe and move, strobe and move, always keeping the gun at the ready, checking each corner and staying aware of one's surroundings, avoiding tunnel vision and watching for movement.

Bolan entered a small choke point corridor, deep in the bowels of Lawang Sewu.

The two-by-four came out of nowhere.

The board smashed painfully into his face, bloodying his nose and knocking him back. The Desert Eagle was torn from his grip as the board clattered to the floor. He reeled, rolling with the blow and grabbing for his Beretta in its shoulder rig. He felt the hot pain of a blade slashing across his rib cage under his arm. When he rolled out and came up on his feet again, his flank was coated in blood.

The Beretta was gone.

The severed straps of the leather shoulder harness hung under his arm. On the floor out of reach was the Beretta, still in its quick-release holster. Above it, tossing the Desert Eagle aside, was the remaining Russian pirate. He held an AK-47 bayonet in his hand and grinned.

Bolan resisted the urge to put his hand to his side. The injury had been done. Letting the enemy know just how badly he had been hurt would do him no favors. All of the Russians, so far, had been talkers. He was familiar with this malady; it befell many a man who'd turned to evil and then saw his life flash before him as his time grew short. With the police closing in and the entire grand plan of Olminsk's a failure, this man, too, knew he was almost done.

"One of Olminsk's countrymen?" Bolan said. He slowly drew the knife from its sheath inside his waistband. The long, partially serrated blade looked lethal in the dim light of the corridor.

"Indeed," the Russian answered, smiling again. "I am Timofei. You may call me death."

"I don't think so."

"No?" Timofei began to circle Bolan in the tight space of the corridor. The bayonet was bright in the low light, its edge keen and slightly red with fresh blood. The Executioner could feel hot wetness soaking his flank and knew that he would need medical attention soon. Blood loss would eventually weaken him. He could not afford to let this go on too long.

The Russian had a hatchet face and cold, dark eyes. "You have been fucking up the works for some time, *dah?*" he asked mockingly. "Who are you?"

"Cooper," Bolan said, answering the man's second question. "It's all finished." After fighting through most of Olminsk's crew, he felt like he'd been through all this before. "Listen to me, Timofei. Doing this now won't change anything."

"It will not?" Timofei feigned innocence.

"Olminsk is gone. The Theta-Seven is destroyed. The pirates you hired to help you are dead or captured. It's over."

"Then I have nothing to lose, *dah?*"

"Just your life."

"I do not think so," Timofei said. "No, I think you are the one who will die. I have disarmed you easily."

Bolan gestured with the knife. "I am armed well enough."

"We shall see." Timofei laughed. Bolan saw his muscles tense and knew the knife-fighter's gambit was coming. "And perhaps—"

The Russian struck in midsentence, hoping to catch Bolan off guard. He thrust with his blade. Bolan sidestepped, slashing at the incoming arm, missing but driving the Russian off balance with the surprise counter. Timofei came around again, slashing a figure-eight pattern through the air, trying to distract the Executioner with useless movements.

He obviously fancies himself quite the bladesman, Bolan thought, and likewise was accustomed to dealing with relative amateurs. That was not unusual among his type. Few would-be knife fighters encountered many like themselves, for the sensible fighter didn't duel with blades. There were too many things that could go wrong to play games like that.

Timofei made a series of grand slashes and parries, all elaborate, all flowing in a style Bolan did not recognize. It appeared to be a series of different disciplines. As Bolan watched, Timofei shifted his knife from forward to reverse grip and back again.

"You are impressed," Timofei said. "I can tell."

"I'll let you know," Bolan said.

"You are," Timofei said confidently. "You cannot help but be. I am the best."

"I've met plenty who thought so."

"And how did you survive against so many skilled fighters, American?" Timofei slashed forward and backhand, carving an *X* in the air. Bolan dodged and counter-slashed, missing Timofei's arm but pushing him back, creating combat stretch between them. Timofei snarled, beginning to grow frustrated. That was good. The more impatient he became, the more reckless he would become, eager to end the fight. That bred carelessness. In a duel with a sharp edge, even a fraction of a section was enough to convert your opponent's lack of attention to his imminent death.

"Now you die!" Timofei screamed. He plunged in, stabbing the bayonet overhand, trying to drive it down past Bolan's defenses. Bolan countered with a fleeting upper block, drawing his arm back and circling around before Timofei could slash the blocking arm. This appeared to enrage him further. He had likely hoped to lure Bolan into a block that he could use to wound the other man, hastening the wounded soldier's blood loss and leaving him further off balance. Instead he had missed his opportunity, and it enraged him.

He swore, taking another broad swipe at Bolan. The soldier checked and parried with his support hand and the spine of his blade, managing to score a backhand blow with the butt of the knife. He hit Timofei in the neck, causing the man to gag and back off a bit.

"Give up," Bolan said, knowing this would only provoke the Russian. "I can see you're getting tired. There's no shame in it. Give up, and I'll take you in."

Timofei screamed and lunged. The Executioner stepped back, at a forty-five-degree angle, and let the blade pass. As it did so he chased it with his own blade, slashing and checking, carving Timofei's knife arm and bringing his blade up and around the limb. As Timofei shrieked, Bolan shoulder-checked him, planting a foot in the Russian's calf and pushing, sending him to one knee. Bolan smashed the Russian on the back of the head with the butt of the knife, knocking him senseless. His eyes rolled up for a moment as he staggered.

The gunshot, when it rang out, took the Russian in the chest. His eyes grew wide as he fell flat on his back, never knowing or comprehending why he had lost. He had been killed twice, in effect—once by his defeat at Bolan's able hands, and once by his unseen foe.

Bolan was very still. He gauged the presence, his knife still in his hand, and risked turning his head to view this new enemy.

The Saudi stood, his sunglasses folded into a pocket of his double-breasted suit. He held a CZ automatic leveled at Bolan's chest.

"Bravo, American," he said. "I would clap, but I do not think that is wise."

"You're Gafar," Bolan guessed.

The Saudi looked surprised. "You know me?"

"I do now."

"Oh, well played," he said. The CZ never once moved. He took a step closer, jerking his chin to the dead Russian. "They were a cast of…what do you call them…*cartoon* characters, yes?" He laughed. "This one thought himself a knife man. The other, a Russian bear. Still another, a *cowboy,* of all things."

"What do you want here, Gafar?"

"I?" Gafar asked. "I am simply cleaning up the mess."

"It's over," Bolan said yet again. "The chemicals are destroyed."

"And so simply, too." Gafar shook his head, his eyes never leaving Bolan's. "Fire. To think the solution was there all along, yet we did not see it."

"Why didn't you?"

"Either treachery or miscommunication," Gafar volunteered readily enough. "The team that originally created the weapon told us that explosion or fire would start the nerve gas reaction. All this time we sought a chemical neutralizer, or some sort of process we could use, to render the chemicals inert. And all along all we had to do was burn them. I do not know how this came about. The original team may have lied. They may have made a mistake. Or some report might have contained an error."

"Why not ask the inventors?"

"Because they were long dead, of course," Gafar said. "You know that, or would suspect that much. You are not stupid. Do you think we would let such people live, after they created something of such power?"

"Left you with something of a problem, though," Bolan said.

"Indeed it did." Gafar sighed. "But the decisions made at the highest levels are not always those with which I agree." Bolan watched the Saudi carefully. Beneath his feigned casual nature was a simmering rage. It was evident in his eyes, in the tightness of his shoulders, in the way his knuckles were white as he maintained a death grip on his pistol. Death waited for Bolan at the other end of the gun's barrel, and this Gafar might or might not be eager to deal it.

"How did you get in here?" Bolan asked, trying to distract him.

"I have *been* here," he said. "The place is laced with switchbacks and secret rooms. Did you know the locals believe it to be haunted? I am not surprised they do. I see ghosts everywhere in these many rooms, behind these many useless doors. This is a place of death. How fitting, that you should meet it here."

"Why hide here?" Bolan persisted.

"Someone had to stop the fool Olminsk from destroying a city," Gafar said. "It was clear to us that he was mad.

You may not have realized just what he was capable of doing, how far he was willing to go, but my government has been studying him for longer, trying to locate the chemicals before he was ready to sell or use them. I thought it very likely he would try to commit suicide. Thus, I brought this." Gafar produced a small electronic device.

"What is it?"

"A portable jammer," Gafar said. "It is Russian in origin, like Olminsk's gear. I have had it deployed since before he got here. As soon as we received word that he was moving on Tugu Muda, I knew this was the logical place for his operation. You made the same assessment, yes? That is how you knew to show up here and make your fire. I am surprised you did not burn the place down. It smells of ash."

"I did make that determination, yes."

"I thought as much. Olminsk's charges could not have detonated, not remotely, as long as this was here and active." He switched the unit off and tossed it aside. It hit the floor somewhere with the sound of cracking plastic. "Now it is useless, so much refuse. Like what is left of my life."

"Your government and mine have a lot to talk about," Bolan said. "It could start with you giving up. Turning yourself in."

"Do you think I am worried about that?" Gafar said. "Did you think I came here to duel you, like that fool?" He jerked his chin once more to Timofei's body. "Do I look like one for grand gestures?"

"I wouldn't know."

"I am here for my nation," Gafar said. "Can you imagine what would have happened had Olminsk succeeded in destroying this city?"

"Saudi Arabia likely would have been blamed," Bolan said.

"Likely?" Gafar scoffed. "All one hears is how many

of your 9/11 hijackers were Saudis. Imagine how much worse it would grow for us on the world stage if a Saudi terror weapon were used to kill a million or more innocent people!" He lowered his pistol, letting the weapon hang loosely at his side in a casual grip. "No, this had to be stopped. It had to be stopped here and now. It should have been stopped by me. Now…my brother is dead. I have failed and my family's life will be forfeit. My own life is likewise forfeit."

"We could give you asylum," Bolan said.

"Asylum?" Gafar looked incredulous. "From what? My own deeds? The reality that my family is destined for the sword? Their heads will leave their shoulders within the week, I suspect. And I will be there to greet them, when they reach paradise. Or not. I have never truly believed. It does not matter. It is finished."

"Wait," Bolan said.

"No, American," he said. "You have done enough, and I have done all I can. Perhaps we should have fought on the same side. You have managed to kill all of my men. You have killed my brother. In defeating me, you have killed *me*. In failing in my duty, I have killed my family. That is the end of the circle."

"Don't," Bolan said.

Gafar put the barrel of his gun under his chin and pulled the trigger.

The gunshot echoed through the empty corridors of Lawang Sewu, leaving Gafar's ghost to join the others collected there.

18

The sea beckoned Vadim Olminsk. On the bridge of the *Milaya Volya,* recently rechristened the *Bonny Lass,* he contemplated the future. His thoughts were dark. He fumbled his pack of cigarettes, finally managing to light one with shaking fingers. He had not yet managed to get his hands to stop shaking. He suspected they would, in time. Brushes with one's own death did that, he supposed.

The insipid new name of his ship bothered him, but it had been necessary. It was supposed to be bad luck to rename a ship, he knew. Olminsk was not overly superstitious. The new crew he had hired on in Jakarta was probably the usual superstitious lot, but they would never know the difference. To their knowledge, the ship had always been the *Bonny Lass,* and Olminsk had always been Fyedor Porevski, a veteran freight captain with a clean record and few ambitions.

How far he had come, only to fall again.

He supposed it was better than dying at the hands of the demon American or those fighting with him. He had not, in fact, expected to escape so cleanly, or so easily. After sneaking way from the disaster at Lawang Sewu, he had gone to the safe deposit box he kept under the Porevski name in a local Semarang bank. There he had removed the credentials that, painstakingly purchased from a counterfeiter years before, would give him the second chance he so desperately needed. He would be tempted to congratulate himself for his foresight, if not for his ire at how much he had lost in the bargain.

A little paint and some forged registration papers had made it possible to remake the *Milaya Volya*. He had some cash tucked away in the safety deposit box, enough to fund his hasty escape with a skeleton crew of contractors. Once in the port city of Jakarta, he had, from long habit, known instinctively which dives and sanctuaries to plumb for the dregs of the city's seagoing men. As with the pirates before them, Olminsk's new crew was easily swayed by promises of easy money, easier women, and some small amount of power taken behind the barrels of guns. Were Olminsk not so dependent on their miserable natures, he would be tempted to despair at the state of human beings so easily bent to raping, pillaging and other acts of barbarism on the seas.

As it was, he needed them.

So far they had managed to take a couple of fishing vessels, one of which had a woman aboard who had afforded the crew a few nights' entertainment. That had been good, Olminsk supposed. It was nothing like the retirement he had envisioned for himself. While he could continue to ply the trade at which he was now so experienced, he doubted he would ever again have the chance at a payday like the one the Saudi chemical had offered. He had lost all the men he trusted from the old days, every one of his former officers. He supposed he regretted that, though shooting Vasily himself had not caused him to lose any sleep. Still, his former crew and friends from the navy had always made him feel nostalgic. He would miss having them around, despite the fact that they had proven unreliable in the end.

To have escaped with his own life was enough, he decided.

There would always be the sea, at least. He could take heart in that. Olminsk drew deeply on the cigarette. He exhaled, then breathed deeply of the salt air, the hot and cold contrast of the smoke and air giving him some measure of the thrill it always had.

He had followed the news with interest. However it was leaked, word that the Saudis had created a terrorist weapon eventually hit the media. Rumors of attacks in Semarang were supported by numerous eye witnesses. The governments of Indonesia and the meddling United States were said to be in emergency diplomatic talks with Saudi Arabia, though to precisely what end was not known by any of the chattering heads on the twenty-four-hour news channels. Reading between the lines, it seemed that world opinion had turned against the Saudis. The United Nations was getting involved. Before it was over, the Saudis would likely be forced to make concessions or reparations of some kind. Exactly what this might be was not clear. Olminsk did not really care.

He had chosen to disappear as much to escape official punishment as to escape death at the hands of the al Qaeda splinter group with whom he had been dealing. He had kept their money, after all, and had failed to deliver on his promise of great and terrible destruction for which they could take credit. They had not, predictably, tried to take credit for the failed attack. The blame for the use of the chemicals had fallen in equal measure on the Saudis and on Vadim Olminsk. The news channels had been running alerts on piracy and its prevalence in the area for days.

While Vadim Olminsk might be wanted by many governments and many other dangerous men, Fyedor Porevski had a clean slate. For this, he was grateful. It would have to be sufficient.

A stiff breeze blew up. The Russian captain grabbed at his hat and tried to keep it on his head. The wind grew stronger, and his cap was torn from his fingers, blown into the unforgiving sea. Much to his surprise, the wind did not diminish, instead growing still stronger as it whipped his coat about him.

Terrified, he gripped the rail with thoughts of a sudden storm and shipwreck in his head. Then he heard the sound.

Descending from the gray clouds above was a large, black helicopter, its whirling blades ripping at him with the force of the air they whipped about. Olminsk looked up, shaking one fist while clinging to the rail.

What were the fools doing? Surely there were regulations regarding—

Olminsk saw the rappelling line snake downward from the chopper. Then he knew.

They had found him.

THE EXECUTIONER descended headfirst on the line, a suppressed Heckler & Koch MP-5 held before him.

It had taken more than two weeks to track Vadim Olminsk. Stony Man Farm's computer team had put in the extra time to sleuth out all of the subtle ins and outs of Olminsk's financial dealings. They had eventually uncovered a record of a safe deposit box, which had prompted a visit from local intelligence operatives. With the name and registration records provided by the bank, Kurtzman and his team had started several system traces. As Olminsk began using his new alias, he left minute data points. These points were found, collected and reported by the Stony Man super-processors, and the Russian pirate captain's trail was slowly pieced together.

Neither Kurtzman nor the local intelligence agencies were able to determine what Olminsk's ship registry might be. Without the ship's name, it had been necessary to comb the local ports for anyone who had seen—or been recruited by—a Russian captain or those working for him. More false leads than Bolan would have expected were generated through this approach. It seemed there were more than a few dispossessed former Soviet and Russian naval operatives trading on the seas in this part of the world.

As the search went on, the fallout from the Semarang operation continued. Brognola relayed word that one Pramana Suharto had been promoted to a position of high prestige within Indonesia's intelligence agency. He had also received some sort of decoration for service to his country. Through channels, Suharto had passed his thanks to Bolan, and his sincere desire that it would never again be necessary for Suharto to work with him. Bolan had taken it in the spirit Suharto had intended.

Relations with the Saudis had run hot and cold, according to Brognola, as relayed through his contacts within the State Department. The royal family was eager to distance itself from the international disaster that had been averted and would take no responsibility for any part of it. Thus, while they apologized for the problems created by "rogue factions within their bureaucratic infrastructure," they admitted to no explicit guilt.

Brognola theorized that, behind the scenes, certain deals were being cut, guaranteeing that the curious love-hate, ally-enemy relationship between the United States and Saudi Arabia would continue. Likely the Saudis were cutting similar backroom deals with those whom their weapon had directly affected, including the Indonesians and elements within the United Nations.

The U.S. Congress had held a series of hearings on the now-hot issue of global piracy. These had been spearheaded by Congressman Jim McAfferty, whose own wife and daughter had been taken hostage aboard the *Duyfken Ster.* The taking of the *Duyfken Ster* and its liberation by unnamed counterterrorist forces had captured the nation's fleeting interest.

It had taken some doing, but eventually the *Bonny Lass* had been identified and its course determined. While taking Olminsk would not do much to eliminate the persistent problem of piracy in the region, it would be one less group of predators on the seas. More importantly, taking out Olminsk would close this particular operation.

The Executioner shot down the line like a striking hawk. When the deck of the *Bonny Lass* loomed beneath him, he jerked back, bringing his combat boots under him and releasing the zip-line harness. The assembly came free and he dropped heavily to the shifting deck of the Russian captain's ship.

Mack Bolan looked like an avenging wraith in his combat blacksuit, balaclava and full harness that bore his personal weapons. He hit the secondary deck hard, leaping down from the upper platform. His eyes were protected behind tinted goggles, which gave him a clear view of the scene before him. The ship was not large, but it was covered with barriers where enemies could hide—rigged equipment, shipping containers and outcroppings in its structure. He ventured forward carefully, a lone hunter bent on justice.

Already, Olminsk's pirate crew were surging to respond to his orders. They rushed up from belowdecks, rifles in their hands, firing blindly and with little effect as the seas moved the deck back and forth. The Executioner calmly held his ground. He triggered first one, then another burst from the MP-5, the short blasts of subsonic 9 mm slugs almost inaudible against the noise of the sea and the chopper overhead. One pirate went down after Bolan stitched him across the chest. A second snapped backward as he was clipped in the head. A third saw the deaths of the first two and, beyond reason, threw down his rifle and pitched himself overboard.

Bolan took the nearest companionway belowdecks. He switched on the tactical light in the foregrip of his MP-5, the barrel of the weapon moving constantly, tracking with his eyes. One of the pirates leaped from hiding with a large wrench in his hand, intent on smashing it into the Executioner's head. Bolan shot him down where he stood. The wrench rang on the metal deck plates.

Bolan did not know where to find Olminsk, specifically, but on a ship this size there were only so many places a man could run and hide. All fugitives, instinctively, went to ground. Aboard this handysize freighter, that would mean descending lower and lower, into the depths of the ship. Bolan followed both his nose and the MP-5, stalking Vadim Olminsk.

He found the Russian captain cowering in the ship's engine room.

"Wait!" Olminsk said. He held a long-barreled revolver but set it very carefully aside, perhaps sensing that time had finally run out. "We can cut a deal! Money! Women! Do not kill me. Let me go, and we can work together! There is much I can do!"

"Somehow," Bolan repeated, recalling their earlier conversation, "I don't see you living a long and fruitful life."

A look of horror and recognition filled Olminsk's features.

Holding the barrel of the MP-5 on target, Mack Bolan reached up and peeled off his goggles and face mask. He stared with cold fury at the man who had caused so many good people to die violent deaths.

"You!" Olminsk choked.

"Me," Bolan said.

"Wait, please, American," the Russian whined. "I was…sick. I was not in my right mind. I am better now."

"Then you must be racked with guilt over the horrible crimes you tried to commit," Bolan told him.

"What?"

"You heard me," Bolan said. "You are going to pay for your crimes. The people your pirates raped and murdered might rest more peacefully, if you do."

"I told you," Olminsk whimpered. "It is not my fault. I was—"

"Sick," Bolan said. "Yes, I know what you said."

"Please," Olminsk begged. "I am not responsible for the terrible acts committed by those working for me. I was a pawn! A captain cannot be responsible for all his crew. How could I control them? It was all I could do to escape them and start my life again. An honest living, American!"

"Rape and murder," Bolan said. "An honest living? No, Olminsk. You'll never victimize another human being."

"You are simply waiting for an excuse to kill me!"

Bolan unclipped the MP-5 from his harness and placed it on the deck. "It's over," he said.

Olminsk's eyes flashed angrily. He grabbed for his gun, swinging the long barrel up at Bolan.

The Executioner's .44 Magnum Desert Eagle flashed from its holster, filling his fist and rising on target in a single, fluid motion. The triangular muzzle belched fire. The blast was impossibly loud in the metal cavern of the engine room.

The mask of fear and denial forever etched into Vadim Olminsk's gray face was a fitting epitaph. The Russian toppled to the deck. The revolver fell from his hand, unfired.

Mack Bolan stood over the dead man.

He keyed his radio, calling the chopper overhead.

"It's done, Jack," he said. "I'm coming home."

Don Pendleton
SKY SENTINELS

**A new spark in the Middle East could ignite
the ultimate global conflagration....**

Iran is flexing its military muscle, kidnapping
U.S. journalists and openly daring America to retaliate.
When Iranian intelligence officers kidnap three prominent
Americans from D.C., Stony Man gets involved.
Dispatched to free the hostages and get a handle on
the main event, Stony Man discovers the planning
stages of a radical multinational plot that could
ignite the next—and last—world war.

STONY MAN®

*Available October
wherever books are sold.*